KARA R. HUNT

PAPER DOLLS

EVE

By Kara R. Hunt

DEDICATION

Dedicated to the One Who paid the price for it all, so I wouldn't have to.

BOOKS BY KARA R. HUNT
FICTION:
The Habakkuk Series
Book 1 - *Paper Dolls*
Book 2 - *Paper Dolls: Kite*
Book 3 - *Paper Dolls: Priscilla*
Book 4 – *Paper Dolls: Lydia*
CONTRIBUTING AUTHOR TO THE FOLLOWING
NON-FICTION WORKS:
Marriage Matters
The Names of God
PODCAST
Cheer UP! Podcast

WHAT READERS ARE SAYING

Finding a woman who couldn't relate to any of the themes in Kara R Hunt's expertly crafted novel, Paper Dolls, would be difficult. Wife, mother, daughter, sibling, friend, females struggling with identity, hope, hopelessness, dreams, and dreaded decisions. The intricate plot is a layer-upon-layer of deep emotional entwinement paired with strong Christian values.

Hunt's writing is superb. These characters portray the author's attention to emotion, and motivation, repressing and expressing old trauma, broken dreams, and the deepest, most horrifying fears, making them anything but paper cutouts of people. They are flesh and blood come to life in a memorable, extremely gifted, beautifully crafted story.

Dr. Deborah Maxey
The multi-award-winning author of The Endllng, A Novel
Licensed Counselor and Marriage and Family Therapist

Paper Dolls is filled with all the things that make women's fiction fans sit up and take notice. Family intrigue, a touch of romance, the pain of loss, the joy of reunion, and the uncertainty of life. Walk with these women as they sort out their lives, their families, and their relationships - or at least try.

- Pegg Thomas, Author and Multiple Award-Winning Novelist

I'm hooked on this series ... I read Book One in the Habakkuk series and I knew I had to read Kite's story. It didn't disappoint ... I love how the author reconnected me with the other members of the community that we met in Book One. There's the right amount of intrigue, warfare, and relationship challenges to keep the story exciting. And hang on, because just when you think you know what'll happen next, you don't! Great book from Kara R. Hunt.

- J. Kingston

Priscilla is Book Three in the Paper Dolls Habakkuk series by gifted wordsmith Kara R. Hunt. This is a Christian contemporary women's fiction that is filled with spiritual and everyday life lessons. This is the story of Priscilla King after she marries Barry. She has confessed all of her sordid past to him and that she has found her faith again. Barry is so happy for her, but his adult children are skeptical.

This is a touching book that gave me all of the feels. I loved reconnecting with some of the past characters, my old friends. It was touching to read about the changes and growth in the characters. I love the bonds of friendship shared by this group of women.

Author Hunt has a poetic style of writing that speaks to my heart. I can picture the scenes as I read her vividly descriptive words. The Christian messages are so welcome and needed in today's world.

All fans of contemporary women's Christian books should get this series.

– Nyla Wilkerson

ACKNOWLEDGEMENTS

To everyone who has purchased, read, reviewed, and supported Books 1-4 in this series, a million thank you's wouldn't be enough to show how grateful I am for every one of you. May Book 5 – *Paper Dolls: Eve* be a blessing to you as well.

A SPECIAL NOTE TO MY READERS

This book is a work of fiction. While the characters and the town of Habakkuk are works of fiction, the situations and circumstances they find themselves in are not.

The LORD God is my strength, and he will make my feet like hinds' feet, and he will make me to walk upon mine high places.

- Habakkuk 3:19 KJV

Chapter 1

EVE STOCKTON placed her purse and keys on the kitchen counter and stared at the handwritten note her husband, Philip, had left on the kitchen table.

Her stomach churned.

He was angry.

Rightfully so.

She'd known this day would come. She just hadn't known when.

And she'd hoped she would've been the one to tell him.

But according to the note, someone had beaten her to it.

A loud classical piano tone came from her bedroom. Her cell phone. She hurried up the stairs and answered it.

"Eve, I'm so glad you answered. There's something I need to tell you."

It was Dinah—the adult daughter of her best friend, Lydia.

And also the daughter of Eve's husband, Philip.

"Dinah, now's not a good time. Philip's going to be home any second, and I need to—"

"That's why I'm calling."

Dinah's voice was apologetic and sorrowful—opposite of her normally energetic and confident tone. A thought popped into Eve's mind. "Oh, Dinah." Eve's hand trembled. "Please don't tell me you're the one who—"

"I am."

Eve pressed her lips together. Her words would be full of fury if she responded too quickly, and she didn't want to apologize for them later.

Eve, Lydia, and Dinah knew Philip was Dinah's biological father. DNA samples they'd taken three years ago had confirmed it. The only person who'd been surprised by the results was Dinah. Eve and Lydia had suspected as much since her birth.

That was thirty-three years ago. Months after Philip's "relationship" with Lydia ended and shortly before Eve and Philip married.

Back then, Eve had asked Philip if he was Dinah's father. He'd denied it. Vehemently. Lydia had been a drug addict at the time, and Philip's family had a reputation to uphold. The Stocktons wielded a lot of power in Missouri's political circles. He'd accused Lydia of lying and accused Eve of being a fool for believing her.

Out of fear of losing Philip, she'd dropped the subject of baby Dinah.

But that was then, and this was now.

She was no longer the young, skittish, insecure woman she'd been on her wedding day. So, decades later, when Dinah asked Eve to help her discover the truth, she'd agreed. The samples she'd provided resulted in a ninety-nine point nine percent chance Dinah was indeed Philip's daughter.

Dinah had asked Eve to let her be the one to tell Philip, and Eve had agreed to that as well. She hadn't known it would take Dinah three years to broach the subject with Philip, and she hadn't thought Dinah would do it without letting her know beforehand.

"Why didn't you tell me you were going to do this, Dinah?

You know how hard it's been for me to keep this secret from my husband. But I gave you my word that I would. And I honored that."

Dinah sniffed. "I know, and I'm so sorry. I didn't plan for it to go this way. He took me by surprise when he called this morning."

Philip had called her? He'd still been asleep when she'd left to open the café. "What time did he call?"

"Around eight." She sniffed again. "Shortly after I arrived at Bliss."

Bliss was the event center Dinah owned. It was also a place she'd banned Philip from years before she knew he was her father.

"He'd called to set up a meeting. He wanted to discuss his company doing business with us again. I said no. He asked again and mentioned that he was under pressure from his board to make things right with our event center. He also added that he wanted to apologize to me for his past behavior. I said no again, and he asked why." She let out a sob. "That's when it all came spilling out, Eve. I told him everything." She sighed heavily. "To my surprise, he didn't say much after that. I think he was in shock."

Eve shook her head. As much as she wanted to, she couldn't be mad at Dinah. Philip calling her out of the blue like that, especially when they hadn't spoken in years, and their last form of communication had been through their lawyers, Dinah had every right to be upset and blurt out whatever she wanted to.

But like Dinah, Eve was also surprised Philip hadn't said anything else. The old Philip would've lost his temper and ranted and raved. He would've shouted heated words at Dinah and said horrific things about her mother. Then he would've immediately called Eve and shouted even worse things at her.

That was the type of behavior that had gotten him banned from Bliss in the first place.

But three years ago was also when Eve had decided she'd had enough. He'd threatened divorce multiple times, but Eve was the one who'd officially pursued it. Philip hadn't been expecting that and the shock had caused a change of heart. He'd agreed to seek counseling with their pastor if she stayed. She'd been doubtful, but after a lot of prayer and fasting, she'd decided to give him a second chance. To her surprise, he'd kept his word. He faithfully met with Pastor Greene three times a week and sometimes on Sunday afternoons.

The changes in Philip hadn't happened overnight, but over time, she saw a different Philip emerge. He was a lot calmer and nicer. She'd felt more loved, thought about, and cared for in the last three years than she'd had in the prior thirty years of their marriage.

The note he'd left on the kitchen table had been written with a black permanent marker. In large letters, he'd let her know that he knew about Dinah.

And that he wasn't okay with her betrayal.

Maybe there was still a little of the old Philip left after all.

Chapter 2

Eve paced back and forth in front of the couch Philip sat on.

"I don't understand it, Evie." Philip's eyes followed her movements. "How could you keep a secret like that from me?"

Eve slowed her pace. So far, so good. She'd expected his voice to be louder, his tone harsher. More accusatory than interrogative. She released a breath and glanced at him. He looked more confused than angry, though his jaw tightened as he waited for her answer.

She chewed her bottom lip for a few seconds then said, "I wanted to tell you, but I'd promised Dinah that I wouldn't. She asked that I allow her the time to talk to you about it when she was ready. If I'd known she was going to wait so long, I never would've made that promise."

"You gave her a sample of my DNA, Eve. You didn't think that was something I should've known about?"

She'd given his comb and toothbrush, along with other items of his, to Dinah. "I don't regret what I did, Philip."

He stood and glared at her. Philip had never hit her. The abuse she'd suffered at his hands had been emotional and verbal. But if there was anything that would cause him to upgrade, it would be this.

"Dinah shouldn't have been the one who," he shouted before his eyes softened, as well as the hard lines around his mouth. He then placed the heel of his palms on his temples. "What am I saying? I know why you didn't say anything. You were afraid of how I'd react." He plopped down on the couch. "Honestly, I can't blame you. News like that would've definitely sent me into a rage."

Eve glanced at him again but kept pacing. Philip's grandfather, a former Missouri Senator and the one who'd raised Philip, had died decades ago. However, the Stockton name still wielded a lot of power, especially in Habakkuk. Philip's father, Henderson Stockton, made sure of that. She'd expected Philip to rant about how in the world he was supposed to explain Dinah to his father, but so far he hadn't mentioned his father at all. Habakkuk had never voted Henderson into a political office, but to her father-in-law, that was irrelevant. Respect and power were all that mattered to him.

However, Philip had yet to mention any of that. Years ago, he would've. And if she hadn't divorced him by then, she would've after he found out about Dinah because he would've blamed her for everything. Living with him would've been a nightmare.

But she saw no evidence of the old Philip. He was upset, but more along the lines of her keeping a secret from him than any political shame his family might face. A part of her had always wondered if Philip was just one bad day away from reverting to the previous ways he'd handled things. This conversation gave her hope that the changes he'd made were real. That he'd looked deep into his soul and was appalled at what he saw.

He cleared his throat. "The more I think about it, the more I realize how much I owe you an apology. Before we married, you asked if I was Dinah's father. I lied and told you *no* when I knew it was possible." He lowered his head. "I just thought that if you knew how I'd taken advantage of your friend like that ..."

He didn't finish his sentence. He didn't have to. Back then, it was obvious that he suspected Lydia had shared the details of their relationship with her. He'd denied Dinah was his because he had to make Eve believe Lydia was a liar, so she'd agree to marry him.

Truth was, she would've married him anyway. She was too young and in love to do anything else.

And blind.

"I owe Lydia one, too."

Eve stopped pacing. Surely, she hadn't heard him right. "Come again?"

"I owe Lydia an apology."

Eve's breath caught in her throat. Of all the things she'd thought she'd hear Philip say, that was not one of them. He owed Lydia an apology and a whole lot more, but for him to acknowledge that was mind-blowing.

She looked into his eyes and searched for the slightest hint of mischief, deceit, or dishonesty. There was none. His blue eyes watered. Was he about to cry?

He shifted his gaze from her to the window. A soft orange glow from the setting sun filled their living room. He swallowed hard but didn't say anything. He stared outside until the sun set, and she'd switched on a lamp.

When he still didn't say anything, she closed the curtains and sat on the couch next to him. "What's going on, Philip?"

No response.

"Are you okay?"

He nodded, then shook his head.

"So you're okay, but you're not?"

He nodded again, then looked at the off-white curtains covering the windows.

She laid a hand on the back of his shoulder, and he turned slightly toward her. She studied his side profile. No tears had fallen, but there was no mistaking the sorrow etched into his face. He closed his eyes. "I put Lydia through a lot, Eve."

"I know."

"She told you everything?"

"Yes."

He shifted in his seat and looked deeply into her eyes. *"Everything?"*

She nodded. "We haven't talked about what happened between the two of you in years, but yes, a few months before Dinah was born, she told me everything."

He ran a hand through his hair. It was still thick, but it had been thicker and longer in his younger days, something he'd always been proud of. Now, the dark brown mane was streaked with gray and a whole lot shorter.

"I'd suspected as much." He groaned. "But I'd hoped …"

"That she'd left out some things?"

"Yeah."

"She wanted me to know exactly what I was getting into."

Blue eyes pierced hers. "How can you even look at me?"

She'd asked herself that a million times. It had taken decades for her to learn how to discern the difference between forgiveness and foolishness. When she'd decided on forgiveness, she walked that path and hadn't looked back. He'd made it hard. Extremely hard. But she'd made promises before God with this man, and she'd vowed that she'd give their marriage every possible chance, no matter how long it took.

Until she couldn't take it anymore.

She silently thanked God that He'd intervened. If she'd walked away, she never would've witnessed the miracle sitting across from her. *This* was the man she'd fallen in love with all those years ago. Not the monster his grandfather had turned him into, but the true Philip.

She placed one of his hands in hers. "I'm sorry you had to find out about Dinah the way you did. And I apologize for keeping it from you for so long. If I could do it over, I'd handle it differently."

He moaned and looked down at the floor. "So would I."

She squeezed his hand. "I know it's a lot, but I think you're right. The best way to approach this is with apologies … to both Lydia and Dinah."

"I think Lydia will hear me out, but I've already tried with

Dinah. She doesn't want anything to do with me."

"That's because she's upset right now. And honestly, I don't think she knows how to accept the fact that you're her father. The man you've shown her previously is not someone a daughter would look for in a dad. You weren't someone to be proud of. You've changed, but she hasn't seen that side of you yet. Give her some time."

"She's known about this for years."

"Well, let's just say that she's as stubborn as her father."

He chuckled and lifted his head. "I don't deserve you, Eve. I never have."

She smiled. "I know."

"I still can't believe I have a daughter." He shook his head. "I was shocked when Dinah first told me. Well, I should say when she *screamed* it at me, but after thinking about it all day, I'm glad the truth has finally come out." He paused before continuing. "In a strange way, I feel at peace. Like reality has caught up with something I've been trying to hide from for far too long."

"You knew the truth?"

"No. Not for sure anyway. But there was no mistaking Dinah's resemblance to my mother."

Philip's mother had passed away when he was thirteen. Eve had never met her, but she knew Philip had adored her. When they'd first met, his mother was a topic he loved to talk about. Since Eve had always been close to her mother, she loved hearing stories of how Philip's mom would sit on the floor with him when he was a toddler, and how they'd put one toy car after another on a large, orange race track, and laugh as the cars sped around and around. Or how she'd lovingly coached him during his elementary years for spelling and math bees. And in later years, how she helped him write political speeches for the private prep school his grandfather insisted he attend.

But a few years into their relationship, he stopped talking about her altogether. When Eve asked why, he made a comment about letting go of the past, but he'd always looked sad and lost when he said it.

Eve had seen plenty of pictures of her mother-in-law, especially after she and Philip married, and she spent more time at the Stockton family estate. Dinah was crawling around in diapers at the time, so she hadn't seen the resemblance. Now that Dinah was older, it was unmistakable.

He sighed. "Every time I saw Dinah, it brought everything back. Everything."

"What do you mean?"

"I've attended conferences all over the world, and I've never acted as badly as I have at Bliss."

Eve was aware of that. She'd also thought it odd that he risked his reputation by acting so horribly in his hometown.

"When my company first started scheduling events at Bliss, I had no idea that Dinah O'Keefe was *Lydia's* Dinah. The last name was different. I didn't even know that Dinah O'Keefe was married."

Well, she wasn't anymore, but it put Eve's heart at ease that Philip hadn't noticed Dinah's wedding ring, which she still wore. That meant she hadn't been someone he'd intended to flirt with. Some of the other women on staff at Bliss hadn't been so lucky.

"When I first walked into Bliss, I was thrown by Dinah's resemblance to Mother. It wasn't until months later that I realized who she was. And that was only because Harold told me."

Harold was Philip's business partner and a member of their church.

"When he told me that, my mind immediately started connecting the dots and the possibility, but ..."

"But what?"

He tossed his hands in the air. "I didn't let the process play out. I fought against it. I looked for things to distract me from it. Not only because Dinah was living proof of my sinful past, but because every time I saw her, she reminded me of something I had worked *very* hard to forget."

Eve leaned forward.

"Then I'd become angry. Angry that she reminded me of—"

"Your mother?"

"Yeah, but not just that."

"What then?"

He rubbed his forehead and then placed his elbows on his knees.

Eve waited. He tried to hide his face with his hand, but she could still see the tightening of his jaw and the reddening of his face and neck. His temple pulsed.

What was upsetting him so? Her gut told her it had nothing to do with his past relationship with Lydia. So what was it? What had he worked so hard to forget? And what did any of that have to do with Dinah?

"Philip—"

"I wanted to forget …"

Eve gently squeezed his hand. "Forget what, Philip?"

He pulled his hand away and looked into her eyes. "That my father killed my mother."

Chapter 3

Eve stared at Philip.

A million questions zipped through her mind, but only one made it past her lips.

"What?"

Philip's hands, the same hands that had been holding hers so gently moments before, clenched into fists. "My dad killed her."

Eve sucked in a deep breath and held it. In the past, when she'd heard shocking news, her thoughts would twirl and twist with the intensity of a tornado and leave her just as breathless. Sometimes, she'd even faint. That wasn't going to happen today. She needed answers.

She closed her eyes. *Lord, help me.*

When her breathing steadied, she opened her eyes. Philip was no longer sitting next to her. He'd yanked the curtains open and stared into the August darkness.

His legs were spread apart, his back rigid. Fists still clenched. He looked ready to fight. But who would be his opponent? It wouldn't be his father. The two of them were close. Philip talked with Henderson every day, sometimes twice a day. He'd done that for as long as she'd known him. Eve shook her head. If Philip thought his father had killed his mother, why in the world would he do that?

"Help me understand, Philip. What makes you think your dad is responsible for your mom's death?"

"I don't think it. I know it."

"But how do—"

He pivoted toward her, nostrils flared. "I saw it."

"Saw what?"

"The murder."

She gasped.

"I didn't *see* it with my own eyes." He thrust his hands into the pockets of his gray slacks. "I overheard him talking about it with my grandfather."

"When?"

"Long ago, when you and I were still dating."

"Is that why you suddenly stopped talking about her?"

He nodded.

Eve grimaced. That was *so* long ago. Why hadn't he said anything about this until now?

His grandfather. No doubt that devious demon had something to do with it.

"What happened?"

His hand shook as he raked it through his hair. "Mom was going to leave Dad and take me with her. When he found out, they argued. Loudly. I was two floors above them, and I still heard every word. My grandfather did, too. He intervened, and Mom stormed out and came up to my room. She looked so tired. She'd never been in the best of health, and on that day, it looked as though it had taken every ounce of strength she had just to hold her head up." The hand that left his hair in a spiked mess now scrubbed across his face. "But her voice was strong, and her eyes danced. She'd finally gathered up enough courage to leave Dad, and she told me to pack my things because the next morning, we were leaving the estate."

His eyes darted to the floor. "The following morning, Dad told me she wasn't feeling well. That she was too weak to get out of bed." He shrugged. "I didn't think anything of it at first. I knew she had a weak heart and struggled to get going in the mornings. When three days passed and I still hadn't seen her, I became suspicious and tried to open their bedroom door to talk with her, but Dad wouldn't let me. Shortly after that, my grandfather pulled me aside and told me that she'd died in her sleep."

"Oh, Philip."

"She seemed so fragile the night she was in my room. The argument she'd had with my dad had taken a lot out of her. I didn't think twice when they told me her heart had failed."

He lifted his gaze to her. "But they lied. The doctor, my father, and my grandfather all lied to me. She was poisoned. I'm not sure what she was poisoned with, but whatever it was, my dad was the one who gave it to her."

"Philip, I am so sorry."

"It was about a year after her funeral when I overheard them talking about it. I was furious, so I confronted them. They told me that I was still grieving and that I didn't hear what I thought I had. But I did. I heard it all. They talked about how Mom had known too much, and how Dad feared when she was no longer under his control, that she'd reveal the skeletons in the Stockton family closet. My grandfather had pressured him to do something about it, so he did. He killed her."

Eve swallowed. Henderson Stockton was no saint, but she never would've pegged him as a murderer. Philip's grandfather? Yes. But Henderson had always been kind to her. Well, the word *kind* was a stretch, but he'd never talked down to her like Philip's grandfather had. However, she kept her distance from Henderson. She always sensed there was something cold beneath the charm he oozed. Unlike Philip's grandfather, she never knew where she stood with her father-in-law. Philip's grandfather didn't care if the whole world thought he was a snake. Henderson, however, tried to hide his slithering reptilian behavior. Eve shivered. She'd had no idea that murder had also been a part of his repertoire.

She wanted to ask Philip if he ever contacted the police and told them what he overheard. But the look on his face told her he hadn't.

He rubbed the back of his neck. "I didn't know what to do, Evie, so I just jumped in my car and drove for hours. When I returned, Dad tried to talk to me, but I refused to listen. My grandfather was the one who calmed me down. He also said that he understood what I was going through. Then he asked if I'd feel better if he kicked Dad off the estate. I said yes, and the next day, Dad was gone." He sat on the couch next to her. "But after a few days, I convinced myself that they were right. Mom's death had to have been a result of her illness. No way would my father have killed my mom. He loved her." His lips tightened. "But a part of me always knew that he loved himself a whole lot more."

He frowned. "I don't know why I bought into their lies, but I do know what I heard." Eve wrapped her arms around his waist, and he leaned his head on her shoulder. "What do I do now, Evie? I can't keep this secret any longer. It's ruined my life, and it almost ruined our marriage. I've let my mother down. The truth was staring me in the face the whole time. She was the most important woman in my life, and I didn't even stand up for her."

Eve wiped a tear away from her cheek. "What would you like to do?"

"I'd like to stand up and be the man she raised me to be."

Eve nodded. "So, are we going to get the police involved?"

He swallowed. "Yeah." He straightened and pulled his phone out of his pocket. "Do you have the non-emergency number?"

"Yes, but are you getting ready to call them right now?" Her voice was higher than she'd intended it to be. "You're not going to talk to your dad first?"

He shook his head. "He'll panic and start calling in favors. Any investigation that might take place would be squashed before it even got started." He cleared his throat. "Besides, if I don't do it now, I never will. My mom deserves justice. I've kept my head in the sand for far too long." He placed a hand on her thigh. "I'd love nothing more than to have you by my side as I do this. But if it's too much, too soon, I understand. I've been tormented for decades by what happened, but this is all new to you. I won't get upset if you'd rather not get involved, but I need to do this while I have the courage."

She scrolled through her cell phone with her free hand and texted him the number. Before he opened it, she pulled him closer and looked into his eyes. "I'm not going anywhere, Philip. I'm here for you."

"Are you sure? Because when Dad finds out what I've done, there's no telling what he might do. We both know he's not above destroying you and everything you've worked for in the process. It could get ugly."

"A woman has been murdered, Philip. You have to tell the police what you know— regardless of the cost."

"It's not me I'm worried about."

Her eyes watered. He cared for her. Maybe he always had, but over the past year, he'd allowed himself to be vulnerable enough to show it. She wiped a tear from her cheek and smiled.

"I know. But it's not just you and me in this fight. You've been a believer for a couple of years now. We're not in this alone. God is with us."

He looked at his phone. "Good, because I know my dad. And when he finds out that I've betrayed his trust, all hell is going to break loose."

Chapter 4

Eve tightened her bathrobe and switched on the coffee maker. The time on the digital display read four a.m.

She sighed.

A full hour later than she usually woke up. She liked to arrive at the café at five, an hour before it opened for the breakfast rush at six. Her regular morning routine was coffee, devotions, and quiet time with the Lord. After that, she showered, dressed, and headed to work at the small but booming café she'd purchased from her mother.

Mom. She needed to call her. Kay Locke retired to Florida three years ago, but she still kept up with what was happening in her hometown of Habakkuk.

A friend had shown Kay how to receive breaking news alerts from Habakkuk on her cell phone. She'd read about Philip's dad before Eve had the chance to tell her. And she immediately purchased a plane ticket to be by her daughter's side.

It hadn't been easy, but somehow, she'd managed to talk her mother out of rushing to her side. For years, Philip had tried to ease the tension between him and Kay. For Eve's sake, her mother had accepted Philip's apologies, but when he'd asked for her forgiveness in regards to how he'd treated them over the years, she hung up on him.

The last thing Eve wanted was her mother hovering over her while she tried to support her husband.

And he definitely needed her support.

It had been a week since Philip had contacted the police.

A week since homicide detectives had taken Philip's statement.

A week since she'd expected Henderson Stockton to storm through their front door.

But he never did.

And he never called. Eve wasn't sure what to make of it.

The past couple of nights had been filled with tossing and turning and very little sleep.

The coffee maker gurgled, and the display flashed bright green. She poured the steaming brew into her favorite cinnamon-colored mug.

She leaned against the granite countertop, wrapped her hands around the mug, and flinched. It was too hot to hold, but she didn't let go. She let the heat seep through her hands and warm her entire body.

Why hadn't Henderson called?

He hadn't been arrested. Not yet, anyway, but an investigation had been launched. At first, all the detectives wanted to do was talk to Henderson, but he refused. He also blocked them from entering his home.

A search warrant was issued and the detectives were given access to the entire Stockton estate. Files had been seized, as well as computers and other electronic devices. Local news channels had been on the scene, and a few reporters had even attempted to interview him.

Henderson was eager to oblige them, but his attorneys quickly put a stop to that.

The day the estate was searched, Philip had been a wreck. He hadn't expected his father to confess to murder, but he'd hoped he'd at least agree to cooperate with the investigators. An order issued by a judge and a massive search of his family home was not only bad news for his dad, it was bad news for

Philip as well. He had already been under pressure to make amends with local establishments and business owners from his board members, and now this.

Philip had also expected his father to kick in their door. Because for the first time in three generations, he'd done what no other Stockton had mustered up the courage to do.

He'd exposed one of their secrets.

A murderous one.

And now there was talk of exhuming his mother's body.

Eve sat at the kitchen table. Philip shuffled into the kitchen.

He pulled out the chair across from her. "I just heard from Dad."

She set her mug on the table. "At this hour?"

"Yeah." He scratched at the dark hairs on his chin. "The call didn't last long. He just wanted me to know how disappointed he was. And how he'd been blindsided by my betrayal. How he'd been rendered speechless for days over how easily I destroyed his trust. He also mentioned something along the lines of how the investigation might uncover some things he tried for years to protect me from."

"Like what?"

He shrugged. "I don't know."

"What else did he say?"

"Nothing. He hung up after that."

"You didn't get a chance to say anything?"

"No, and it's probably for the best. I have nothing to say to him at this point."

"Philip, you and your dad are pretty close."

"You know, I've been thinking about that. I wonder if all the time we spent together was just another way for him to control me."

"What makes you think that?"

"We never talked about Mom, but we talked about everything else. There's no longer any doubt in my mind that he used our," he made air quotes with his fingers. *'Father-son relationship'* to keep tabs on me. Deep down, I think he knew one day I was gonna say something."

"I'm so sorry, love. I know how hard all of this has been for you."

"One of the things Pastor Greene always said to me, was that there was a lot more to my explosive temper and irrational behavior than I realized. When I'd ask him what it was, he said that if I stayed true to my commitment to Christ, it would be revealed—especially if the cause was hindering my Christian walk.

"In yesterday's session, he mentioned how peaceful I looked." Philip chuckled. "That's when it hit me, and I realized I'd had the keys to the prison I'd been in the whole time, except I didn't know it. All I needed to do was face the truth. When I told him that, he said I'd been a prisoner of war. That I'd been at war with myself and the truth. And that there had been a part of me that just couldn't acknowledge that my father had killed my mother."

She stretched her hand across the table, and he grasped it. "I was upset by the abrupt way Dinah told you she was your daughter. But now, I'm glad it happened the way it did. It has led to a breakthrough for you, Philip. A huge one."

"And hopefully justice for my mother."

"When was the last time you heard from the detectives?"

"Last night, after I left the church. They seized a lot of documents and other electronic files from the estate, but they said it would be a couple of months, if not a year before they could get through it all. And as expected, Dad has denied everything. He told them that I've never been the same since Mom died. And that I knew she had a weak heart, and that I blamed him for causing it." He shook his head. "The way the detective described it, Dad's making me out to be a grief-stricken loon, but I'm not crazy, Evie. I didn't see him kill Mom, but I know I heard him talking with my grandfather about how he did it."

"Then let's pray that they'll find all the evidence they need."

"I want him to spend the rest of his life in prison for what he did."

"I do, too."

Philip clenched her hand and led them in prayer. He prayed for wisdom and strength. He also prayed for his dad. He asked the Lord to minister to Henderson's heart and for the truth about what really happened to his mother to be revealed.

He held on to her hand a few seconds more, then gently kissed it before letting go. She smiled and glanced at the clock. She had thirty minutes to shower and head to the café.

She looked at Philip. "My car is acting weird again. Sometimes it starts up, sometimes it doesn't. Thomas Automotive has a new location a block from the café. I'll drop it off there this morning, then walk the rest of the way. Will you be able to pick me up this afternoon?"

"Sure. I'm working from home today anyway, but if you drop the car off, you'll be late opening up the café."

She grabbed her phone off the kitchen counter. Mabel Martin, the café's cook and also the mother of her friend, Priscilla, usually arrived twenty minutes earlier than Eve. She texted her and told her she was running late. Mabel replied and told her to take her time and that she'd open up for her.

Eve kissed Philip on the cheek. "Mabel's going to take care of that for me."

He kissed her hand again and smiled, but his eyes looked sad.

"Philip, I can stay if you want me to. I'll just text Mabel again and tell her I decided to take the day off instead."

"I'll be fine after a cup of coffee."

"Are you sure?"

He nodded. "I'll go for a run before the coffee." He stood and kissed her on the lips. "I know it's a short distance from Thomas Automotive to the café, but please be careful. I've seen a homeless man sleeping between some of the buildings."

Eve waved away his comment. "Oh, that's just Mr. Hale. He's harmless."

"Mr. Hale?"

"He was one of my professors at the state university."

His brows raised. "That was a long time ago, Evie. People change."

"He was a regular customer until about a year ago. He lives with his granddaughter. He's close to ninety now and still sharp as a tack. However, he doesn't like being a burden to his granddaughter so when it's warm out, he roams the streets of Habakkuk."

"That's not safe."

"She doesn't like it, but she says it's easier than fighting with him about it. When it gets cold, she scoops him up and takes him back to her place."

"Huh." Philip chuckled. "I always thought he was too well-dressed to be homeless. The trench coat and tennis shoes looked a bit rough, but the shirt and pants were designer. They were filthy, but you could still tell they were well-made." He looked into her eyes. "I know you know him, but still be careful, okay?"

"I will."

In the bedroom, she tossed her robe and pajamas onto the bed, then quickly showered.

After pinning her damp hair to the nape of her neck and leaving a few tendrils loose to soften the lines around her face, she stepped into her closet and pulled on a light blue sleeveless denim dress. It buttoned down the front and fell comfortably below her knees. She completed the ensemble by adding a wide, bright red leather belt and matching sandals.

She looked in the mirror and smiled.

It wasn't that long ago when she'd been described as dowdy or frumpish. She hadn't been confident in herself or how she looked, and apparently, she'd presented herself to the public that way as well.

But once again, that was then, and this was now.

She wasn't *exactly* sure when she'd become aware of her own value, but she knew who was responsible for it.

Roger.

Her former music producer.

For as long as she could remember, singing, writing, and recording praise and worship music had been her refuge. She'd written her fair share of love songs as well, but when she'd made up her mind to divorce Philip, her girlfriends had let it slip that her music producer—someone they'd all been friends with since their college days—had secretly been in love with her for years.

She thought for sure they'd been mistaken. Who in their right mind would have a decades-long secret crush on her? Curious, she asked Roger about it. When he didn't deny it, something inside her changed.

Unlike Philip, someone had actually *wanted* to be involved in a romantic relationship with her. Thought she was worthy of that kind of love. No strings attached and no pressure from family members. Roger had wanted to be with her simply because of who she was.

He'd honored her marriage by never saying anything to her about it. But that warm afternoon, with the sun shining through her windshield and a breeze coursing through her car windows, she fell in love.

With herself.

As Roger Roarke shared why he was in love with her, she was touched by his words and sentiment, but they also made her angry.

For decades, she'd longed to hear the words coming out of Roger's mouth, to have come out of Philip's.

But back then, the only words Philip had for her were full of ridicule and disdain.

Words that had eroded her confidence, one painful jab at a time.

Philip only married her because his grandfather had told him to.

Roger had *wanted* her to be his wife.

She never felt wanted in the prior years she'd spent with Philip.

And with her divorce pending, she'd seriously considered moving on with Roger. In all the years they'd known each other, he'd never said an unkind word to her. She already loved him—as a friend—but she wasn't *in* love with him. However, she couldn't deny that it wouldn't have been that hard to transition from the former to the latter.

And perhaps she would've if Philip hadn't begged her to give him a second chance.

Unbeknownst to Eve, Philip had known for years how Roger had felt about her. Roger had told him months before she and Philip tied the knot. But Philip was on a mission from his grandfather, and he turned a deaf ear to anything Roger had to say about Eve.

Roger then took her aside and tried to share with her how he felt and how she deserved someone, *anyone* better than Philip. But it didn't take Roger long to realize that Eve wasn't listening either.

She'd only had eyes for Philip.

It wasn't until many tortuous years later that she realized it took more than one person in a marriage to feel that way.

She reached into her jewelry box, pulled out a pair of tiny gold earrings, and inserted the gilded luminescent hoops into her earlobes.

After she and Philip had reconciled, they'd decided that it probably wasn't the best idea for her to continue to work with Roger. At the time though, she was in the middle of a Christian music album with him. But after they put the finishing touches on the record, they wished each other well and agreed to part ways.

Roger still lived in Habakkuk, and he still owned Roarke's Music Studio, which was just a short drive from their home. Due to Three-Sixteen, a local Christian music band he produced, his business was soaring.

Eve was glad. Only God knew if things would've worked out between the two of them, but she couldn't be happier that things were going well for him. He was a good man.

And she was also glad that Philip had found the good man inside of himself as well. It had taken a while, and she'd had her doubts, but in the end, he'd proven himself worthy.

Of her.

The conversations she'd had with Roger reminded her of all the good things she'd forgotten about herself. No one would ever call her beautiful or even pretty, but she had a good heart and a lot of love. Something Philip had often taken advantage of.

Roger's words had buoyed her confidence, and over time, her outward appearance reflected that.

Philip noticed it as well and eagerly welcomed it.

He was the one who'd surprised her with the red leather belt and shoes, something she never would've purchased for herself. It was more in tune with something her friend Priscilla would wear.

Or so she thought.

After wearing the belt and shoes with other articles of clothing, she quickly realized how adding color to her usually drab brown and dull grey attire boosted her mood. She then purchased several other colorful accessories and updated her wardrobe.

Today, she had to deal with a temperamental vehicle, Mr. Hale—a stubborn old man who she was sure would reject her offer to enter the café to escape the heat, and the long list of questions her customers always seemed to have about her father-in-law.

Why do the police think he killed his wife?

Did he do it?

Was there a body discovered on the estate?

How many other people do they think he might've killed?

As far as she could tell, no one knew that it was Philip who'd spoken to the police. But in a small town, it was only a matter of time.

So be it. For now, she was going to walk boldly into a world that she only recently realized was full of color.

Chapter 5

Eve pulled the door open to Thomas Automotive.

"Hey, Eve."

She smiled and returned Abe Thomas's greeting. He stood behind a makeshift counter. He was a big guy, easily over six feet. Curly red hair peeked beneath a cap that had the outline of a Mustang on it, and he sported a long red beard that lay on top of his stomach.

She walked up to the counter. She wasn't sure what the countertop was made of, but it was clean. The automotive shop was small, but everything from the shiny black seats—which were right by the entrance—to the cork-covered floor was spotless.

She smacked her hands against the counter. "Abe, my car is acting funny."

He chuckled. "Funny acting cars keep me in business. Tell me what it's doing."

She told him, and he quirked a brow. "I have an idea of what the problem may be. Are you headed to the café? I can walk down and talk it over with you later, once I've had a look at it."

"Oh, you're going to be able to get to it today?"

"Look at it, yes." He pointed to a large black ledger on the counter. "Work on it? No. One of my mechanics is out sick. Both of my sons are filling in the hours, but we're still backed up. Do you need it back in a hurry?"

She shook her head. "Philip's been working from home, so I can use his car."

"Give me a few days. I can have it ready by Friday afternoon."

"That'll work. And no need to let me know what's causing the problem. I just want it fixed. I trust you."

He smiled. "I appreciate that. But what about Mr. Stockton? He's a stickler about that type of thing."

"He knows I've been having issues with it, and that I was bringing it in here today. He'll be fine with it."

The look on Abe's face told her that he wasn't so sure. "How about this? If it's over a grand, I'll shoot him a quick text."

Abe had experienced Philip's wrath in the past. Twice Philip's lawyers got involved when he and Philip disagreed on the cost of a repair. The last time Philip pursued legal action, the cost of defending himself almost put Abe out of business, so she understood his hesitation.

But Philip had come to respect her financial decisions. She'd always managed their money well. They were as financially flush as they'd ever been, and Philip was grateful for it. She was tempted to explain that to Abe but handed him the key to her car instead. She needed to get going. "Thanks."

He attached a label to the key and placed it on a wall hook next to the counter. "See you on Wednesday."

"Wednesday? I thought you said the car won't be ready until Friday."

"Right. The car won't be ready until then, but there's no way we're going to miss out on Miss Mabel's Meatloaf Special on Wednesday."

"We're?"

"My boys and I."

Her employees regularly dropped off menus at local businesses. Obviously, Abe and his sons had received one. She laughed and pushed open the shop door. "I'll let her know how much you guys are looking forward to it."

"Please do."

She waved goodbye and made her way across the parking lot, and onto the sidewalk that led to her café.

The sun was bright and the rays warmed her bare arms. She glanced at her watch. It was almost seven-thirty. Wow. She was *really* late. The breakfast rush would now be in full swing.

Sometimes in the mornings, she'd help Mabel with prep, but that was all Mabel allowed her to do in the kitchen. The majority of her day was spent in her office balancing the books, filling out purchase orders, and talking with vendors. She also stayed on top of her employee's work schedules. She'd been blessed with a great staff. In the mornings she had three waitresses who were semi-retired and didn't mind getting up early and working a few hours a week.

In the afternoons, she had five high school students who rotated shifts. Both the older and the younger workers made her job easy. Rarely were there any last-minute schedule or shift changes, and she hadn't received any customer service complaints.

Next door to her café, on the right, was The Gourmet Chocolate Shoppe. In between their two buildings was a narrow alleyway that led to the back of both businesses. It wasn't wide enough for two people to walk side-by-side, but the short brick buildings provided protection from the early morning sun.

At least, that was what Mr. Hale had told her.

She approached the alleyway and peered into it. Mr. Hale was stretched out on the concrete with his back leaning against one of the walls. He'd covered himself with a trench coat.

She wanted to wake him and urge him to come inside, but he was sound asleep. She'd heard his snoring long before she'd reached the alley.

She swung open the door to the café and Mabel's daughter, Priscilla, was sitting in a corner booth. Sitting comfortably in her lap with tiny arms stretched toward Eve was Priscilla's adopted daughter, Heidi, who'd recently turned a year old.

Next to Priscilla were three more familiar faces. Friends she'd known since childhood. Kite Eagle, Lydia Day, and Mary Rabin.

She hurried to the booth, waved at her friends, and scooped up Heidi. In between covering Heidi's face with kisses, and the toddler's giggling, she asked her friends about their surprise visit.

Lydia tilted her head to the side. "We're here for breakfast."

Eve kissed Heidi's nose. The child was too adorable, and her dark skin tone and thick curls matched Priscilla's perfectly. She then turned to Lydia. "You know what I mean."

They laughed, and Priscilla asked, "May I have my baby back, please?"

Eve placed Heidi on her hip. "No."

Priscilla giggled before adding, "Listen, if you knew how difficult it was for me to pull her away from her daddy this morning, you'd have mercy on me."

Heidi's adopted dad was Barry King, Priscilla's husband, and one of the wealthiest men in Habakkuk.

Priscilla continued. "He's been taking her to the office every morning. I have to plead with him *and* her just to spend time with my own daughter." She tsked. "However, the writing's on the wall. She's definitely a daddy's girl."

"Daddy?" Heidi asked. Her brown eyes widened, and so did her smile.

"Oh, no." Priscilla blew out a breath. "What did I say that for?"

Heidi looked around the café. When she didn't see her dad, she frowned, and her eyes rounded and filled with tears. Eve hugged her close. "Oh, sweetie, you'll see him soon. Have you eaten yet?"

She shook her head back and forth against Eve's chest. "Daddy." She sniffed, and her tiny body began to shake.

"Don't cry, sweetie." Eve rubbed her back. "Grandma's

here, and you know how much she loves to make those bunny pancakes for you. Would you like some of those?

Heidi's head popped up. "Bunnycakes?"

Eve nodded and looked at Priscilla, who said, "I'll order her some."

Eve tickled Heidi. "Yay! Guess who's getting bunnycakes?"

Heidi's eyes widened again, and the tears disappeared. She gave Eve a big smile as her dimples sunk unbelievably deep into her cheeks. "Look at that," Eve said, staring at the two tiny white rectangles that had broken through Heidi's gums. "She has more teeth coming in." Eve buttoned a strap on Heidi's pink jumpsuit, then handed her back to Priscilla.

"I know." Priscilla settled Heidi back onto her lap. "But this time they don't seem to bother her as much. So far, she hasn't lost any sleep over them."

Kite pulled a stuffed bunny out of her purse and handed it to Heidi, who screamed with glee before tugging on its long ears. "We are here for breakfast, but we also came to hang out with you, and find out how things are going. How are you holding up with all of the media attention Henderson's been getting?"

She noticed her friend asked how *she* was doing and not Philip. No surprise there. All of them had witnessed first-hand his mistreatment of her. They also knew his behavior had improved since then. However, her friends caring how Philip felt about anything was new to them.

Kite, Priscilla, and Heidi were on the same side of the table, so she slid into the booth next to Mary and Lydia. Her friends had been the first people she'd called after Philip contacted the police.

"I'm doing okay, though we both thought we'd hear from Henderson immediately after the detectives showed up at his house, but he didn't call Philip until this morning."

Mary tensed and looked into Eve's eyes. "What did he say?"

"He wasn't the ranting and raving lunatic we'd expected,

but he did let Philip know how disappointed in him he was."

Kite leaned against the table and whispered, "He didn't deny killing his wife?"

Eve shook her head and kept her voice low. "Only to the police."

"I can't imagine how difficult this must be for you," Mary said. She then tightened her lips before adding, "And I can't believe Philip is just now sharing this information with you."

Eve sucked in a breath. That had been a sore spot for her as well. But she'd seen Philip's face when he'd told her how hard he'd worked to forget what he'd heard. She knew he hadn't intentionally left her in the dark for all those years, but it hurt just the same.

Lydia broke the silence. "Philip going against his dad is new to him. How was he after the phone call?"

Eve's heart warmed. For Lydia of all people to ask how Philip was doing showed how hard Lydia was trying. She wasn't a hundred percent convinced of Philip's change of heart, but she had been praying about her own.

"He's doing a lot better than I expected. He's more relaxed now. Not just physically, but emotionally. Perhaps spiritually as well."

Priscilla stared at the table. "Bringing secrets to light will do that. It's when they're kept in the dark that they do the most damage."

Eve knew that wasn't a dig at Philip. Her friend was sharing the wisdom she'd gleaned from confessing to her mother about her past lascivious lifestyle. It had been difficult, but the strained relationship between the two of them had been restored and made stronger because of it.

However, Eve doubted anything like that would happen between Henderson and Philip. Even though Mabel hadn't been happy about her daughter's lifestyle, neither one of them had been at risk of spending the rest of their life in prison over it.

Henderson was.

He could die there.

She wouldn't lose any sleep over it, but her husband would.

As if reading her mind, Lydia asked everyone at the table to join hands, and she prayed for Philip. Lydia thanked God for the miraculous work He'd done in Philip, asked for Philip's heart to continue to soften, and that his relationship with the Lord would grow stronger during this difficult time. She also prayed for Henderson.

Eve didn't hear much of that part of the prayer. She was still stuck on the "miraculous work" in Philip that Lydia had thanked God for.

She pressed her lips together and muffled a chuckle. Lydia had no idea just how *miraculous* the Lord's work had been. Eve still needed to let Lydia know that Philip wanted to apologize to her. And Dinah.

Lydia wouldn't take her seriously at first, but when Eve assured her she wasn't kidding, she wouldn't be surprised if Lydia fainted.

Miraculous indeed.

Chapter 6

After Philip picked up Eve from work, he suggested a stroll in the park before they headed home.

When they returned, she prepared a quick dinner. The phone in Philip's home office rang just as they were finishing up.

She placed the dinner dishes in the sink and washed them before heading upstairs to Philip's office. He plugged in his computer as he talked on the phone.

He was going to be a while.

She walked down the hall to their bedroom and quietly shut the door.

On the nightstand next to her bed, she kept a spiral notebook and pen. She retrieved them and sat on the bed. All during their walk in the park, the beginning lyrics of a song buzzed in her head. She needed to jot them down before she forgot them.

Who knew
Life with you would turn out so grand
Oh, how quickly it could've ended
I was so offended
But ...
Who knew?

One percent of the love songs she wrote were about the early stages of love, where everything was fresh and new.

The other ninety-nine percent were inspired by her relationship with Philip. Only a few of those songs ever saw the light of day, but this one had promise. She wasn't crazy about the lyrics, but she didn't want them to evaporate into thin air, either. Many times over the years she'd thought her initial lyrics were too cheesy, too sentimental, or too transparent, so she'd rip the paper from her notebook and toss it in the trash, only to retrieve it the next day.

One of the songs she'd thrown away, she'd detested. She sounded way too desperate in that song. And when she retrieved it and put it to music, it sounded even worse. Not only did she sound desperate, she'd come across as needy and clingy.

Nevertheless, she'd presented it to Roger, who was still her music producer at the time. After months of tweaking the piano intro and adding a few lyrics of his own, he gave the song to a young married couple he also produced. Because the couple were particular about the type of love songs they sang, they hadn't gained much traction in the music industry. However, they were both strong vocalists and played a wide variety of instruments. The life they breathed into the song she'd written, blew her away. Their fans loved it. She'd had no idea the song would pluck and prod at the emotions of so many people.

The name of the song was *Through Thick and Thin,* and when it was released, it quickly rose to the top of the Inspirational, Christian, Country, Pop, and R&B charts.

Ever since then, she vowed to always retrieve her songs from the trash.

"Hey."

She dog-eared the page she'd been working on as Philip plopped down on the bed next to her. "What are you doing?"

She tapped the pen against the paper.

He smiled. "I should've known." His forehead wrinkled. "Am I a bad guy or a good guy in this one?"

She bit her lip. Should she tell him? Or should she wait until she finished writing it?

"Let's just say I think you're going to be happy with this one. I can't wait to see the look on your face when you hear it, but it may be a while before I finish writing it."

"Good. I'm looking forward to it." He lowered his eyes. "You know, we never did find another music producer you liked. Are you thinking about submitting this one to Roger?"

She jerked her head back. "What? No. Why would you ask that?"

He sighed. "Eve, out of the fourteen producers we've interviewed, you've only liked eight of them and worked briefly with five. I thought maybe you'd finally found the right one with Edgar since you worked with him for two months instead of two weeks like the others. But then you ditched him, too."

"I liked Edgar. But the two of us just didn't have—"

"What you and Roger had?"

"Philip."

He lifted his hands. "I'm not trying to start anything, honest." He scratched his cheek. "But you haven't been back inside of a studio in a while now. The last few producers you worked with were good, but as I watched you work with them, I could tell something was off."

"Like what?"

"You and Roger had a vibe."

"Meaning?"

"It was easy between the two of you. You were always relaxed, smiling, and laughing. You'd write a few lyrics and he'd add to them, but the words would sound like they came from you. It was like he was inside of your head gently pulling free the remaining verses. And when you'd sing, he had a way of coaxing out tones and ranges I'd never heard before. The two of you were amazing together."

Everything Philip said was true. However, she had no idea he'd noticed all of that. Especially since she could count the number of times he visited her in Roger's studio on one hand.

She flipped the notebook closed. "Where are you going

with this, Philip?"

"You don't write music as much as you used to. And you don't hum or sing when you're doing stuff around the house anymore." He sighed. "Especially, if I'm around."

"That's because you've always said you hated my singing."

"I love hearing you sing, Evie, but I found it hard to tell you that." He shifted on the bed. "I criticized you so much on everything else, I honestly didn't think you'd believe me."

"I wouldn't have."

"I know. But the point I'm trying to make is that ever since you left Roger, you're not as creative as you used to be." He pointed to the notebooks. "You used to have tons of those things lying around the house, filled cover to cover with lyrics. You don't sing and you don't write anymore and it's my fault. I miss that side of you and that's why I called Roger."

She squinted at him. "You did what?"

"Even if you had agreed to work with one of the other producers, I knew it never would've been able to compare to what you and Roger had, and I feel responsible for that. I mean, it wasn't my fault he fell in love with you, but I knew how he felt about you before we even married. I should've told you. If I had, you never would've agreed to work with him in the first place." He swallowed hard. "The creative vibe the two of you have developed over the years is strong. Roger's a part of your creative process, and you haven't been the same since the two of you parted ways. I wanted to fix that."

Eve opened her mouth and then quickly shut it. She didn't know what to say, but she did know what she wanted to do. She wanted to slap Philip.

"You had no right to call him about that without talking to me first."

"I just called him, Evie, I didn't set up anything." He scooted closer to her on the bed. "Roger and I were best friends. I called him because it was time. He and I never really talked about what happened between the two of you that day. I heard your version of it, but I also needed to hear his."

"What did he say?"

"Exactly what you'd said, except he added some things."

"Like what?"

He looked at the ceiling before answering. "Let's just say, he went deeper. A lot deeper."

Deeper? What did that mean? Roger wasn't a liar, so she knew he wouldn't have made anything up. But what more could he have said?

Philip cleared his throat. "I'm not going to repeat everything he said because it was hard for me to hear, but the things he did share, he'd been wanting to say to me for a long time."

She still didn't understand. "I don't get it. Roger never held back on calling you out on your behavior. Even when he knew you'd rage at him."

"His words were more than his usual lines of what a *fool I've been when it comes to you.*' He reminded me of," he cleared his throat again. "Just how special you were to him."

Eve was speechless. Roger had told her husband how *special* she was? That was inappropriate and could've landed her in really hot water with Philip. Destroyed *everything* that the two of them had overcome in the past year.

But part of her wanted to smile. She tightened her lips because that would've been even more inappropriate.

"Evie, during my conversation with Roger, I realized how dangerously close I came to losing you. He shared things with me that he never would've shared with you. His feelings for you run deep. I'm not sure he'll ever stop loving you."

She remained silent.

He bowed his head. "How do you feel about that?"

"I don't want to talk about this, Philip."

He reached for her notebook and pen and placed them next to him on the bed. "Sweetie, I'm not mad at you or Roger, but I would like to know how you feel about him."

"Why?"

"Because you lost thirty years of happiness by staying by my side. You deserve better than that. I can't change the past, but I can make sure that you never have to go through that again. And if that means I need to step back and—"

"Don't finish that sentence."

"Eve." His voice shook.

"Don't."

He reached for her hand and stared at it before raising his eyes to hers. When he opened his mouth to say something, she shook her head. "Don't say it, Philip."

After a few minutes, he nodded. "So it's you and me, right? Forever?"

"Yes, it is." She kissed his hand. "Forever."

"You promise?"

"I do."

"Good, because there's something else I'd like to add regarding Roger."

She huffed out a breath. "Seriously?"

"Singing and writing music makes you happy. It's a part of who you are. And I'm okay with Roger continuing to be a part of that process."

"What are you saying?"

"If you want to work with him again, I won't have a problem with it."

She yanked her hand away from his. "You won't have a problem with me working with someone who's in love with me?"

"What I'm saying is, if that's a sacrifice I need to make, then I will."

"Are you trying to get rid of me?" She blinked away tears.

"No." He pulled her onto his lap. "Of course, not. I love you. It's you and me, forever." He leaned his head against her chest. "I just want you to be happy and full of joy again. So does Roger. We've agreed to be smart about it and keep it professional. I promise to be there for every session, even if that means taking time off from work. I won't just be a spectator this time. I promise to be more involved. I'm not a producer, and we both know I can't sing or write, but I'll be there for whatever else you need." He pulled her closer and snuggled deeper into her chest. "I promise."

She wiped at a tear that managed to escape. How many years had she longed to hear those words from her husband? His encouragement and support would've meant everything to her.

But did it now?

It did.

She wanted to get back in the studio with Roger. Her creative juices had started flowing again, and she couldn't wait to get his take on the notes and songs dancing around in her head.

But she wouldn't do it. She couldn't.

Roger would continue to be the gentleman he always was, but the difference now was that she knew how he felt about her.

Would she be able to focus so that they'd be able to continue to write chart-topping songs together? Praise and worship songs, sure. But what about the love songs? Would she misread every look and lyric they wrote together?

Would Philip?

Would working with Roger again stir up feelings of "what if?" Any feelings at all would be inappropriate. The question wasn't if Roger would be able to keep it professional, the question was—would she?

"I trust you, Evie."

She smiled. Philip was in tune with her again. It had been years since he'd been able to decipher her silence.

She ran her fingers through his hair and glanced at the notebook and pen next to him. She itched to pick up the pad and write again. It had been way too long since she'd felt that type of inspiration.

He squeezed her waist and looked up at her. "We'll take it one session at a time. If it becomes too much for you, Roger," he rubbed the back of his neck. "Or me, we'll end it. No questions asked."

She felt a wide grin spreading across her face. "Okay."

He chuckled. "See? You're happier already." He handed her the notebook and pen. "I'll leave you alone. I can't wait to see what new songs you and God come up with."

"I can't either."

That is, if God was even a part of this. She hadn't bothered to ask.

When Philip closed the door behind him, she closed her eyes and prayed. "Lord, if it is *not* Your will for me to work with Roger again, please let me know now."

She waited and listened.

Nothing.

But her fingers had already started writing a new song. When she finished, she looked at the words and shook her head.

The lyrics were about Him being a shelter in the storm.

She sighed. What in the world was the Lord up to?

Chapter 7

Eve glanced at the group text that dinged her phone. It was from Abe Thomas. He'd sent the text to her and Philip. Her car was ready.

The clock on her office wall said four p.m. Thomas Automotive closed at five.

She typed out a separate text to Philip, letting him know she would be leaving the café early to pick up her car, and heading home afterward.

He replied with a chef's hat emoji and attached a picture of what looked to be a steaming tray of homemade lasagna.

Philip had cooked?

He'd attempted breakfast a few times, though most of it had been inedible. However, he was good at making sandwiches. That was the extent of his "cooking skills." But homemade lasagna? That had never happened before.

Ever.

She replied with the wow and surprise emojis, along with the word *yum* in capital letters. She doubted it would be, but at least he tried.

However, she should probably grab something to eat before picking up her car.

The café closed every day at two, but Mabel was still in

the kitchen prepping for the morning rush.

Eve shut down her office computer and tucked her phone into her purse. When she hurried into the kitchen, Mabel was slicing onions over a large bowl. "Evening, Mabel. Anything left over from today?"

Mabel laid the knife on the counter. "There's a little bit of chicken salad left."

Eve walked to the refrigerator. "Oh, this looks good." She pulled the container from the refrigerator and unwrapped it. Mabel didn't serve leftovers at the diner. Everything was served fresh. Before heading home, she'd load the leftovers into her car and take them to the church down the street. The church staff loved her food and looked forward to her daily visits.

Mabel handed her a box of Saltines and a spoon. "What's up? Normally, you fix dinner for you and Philip at home. Is he acting up again?"

Eve shoved a cracker loaded with the tasty goodness into her mouth and shook her head. She followed it with another one. Mabel handed her a bottle of spring water. Eve took several sips before speaking. "Oh, Mabel. That was delicious. I'm surprised there were any leftovers."

"The breakfast crowd kept me on my toes, but the lunch crowd was pretty light."

"Well today, I'm grateful for that. Philip made lasagna for dinner, and it didn't look like he picked it up from the frozen section at the store. He doesn't know how to cook, but every time he watches one of those famous chefs on TV, he tries to follow their recipes. Mostly breakfast dishes, but now he's moved on to dinner."

"How does it work out?"

"It doesn't. I eat small amounts, smile, and thank him for trying."

Mabel laughed. "Those TV shows make it look so easy, don't they?"

"Yep." She loaded up three more crackers and bit into them between sips of water. "Sorry about the mess." She placed the spoon and empty bowl in the sink and turned on the hot water. "I'm in a hurry. I need to pick up my car from Abe's before they close."

Mabel grabbed a dish towel and squirted dish soap onto it. "Don't worry about the dishes. I'll take care of them."

Eve hugged Mabel. "Thanks. See you tomorrow. And please give that precious little Heidi a big kiss for me."

Mabel chuckled. "Will do."

Eve exited the diner and locked the door behind her. Dark clouds hovered and threatened to open up any minute. She glanced at the space between her building and The Gourmet Chocolate Shoppe. The alleyway was empty. Good. Hopefully, Mr. Hale had called his daughter when the clouds started to gather.

Raindrops fell intermittently. She quickened her pace. When she stepped onto the parking lot of Thomas Automotive, the rain went from intermittent to pouring. Abe ran out to her with an open umbrella.

"Thanks, Abe."

"Seems like that rain came out of nowhere." He pointed to her vehicle which was parked in a spot near the street. "My son finished it around noon, but I figured you'd want to wait until the café closed to pick it up." They walked quickly to the shop, and Abe yanked open the door as thunder crackled overhead. "Now I wish I would've called you earlier." He let down the umbrella and dashed behind the counter. He returned with a roll of paper towels. "You're soaked."

"It's not too bad." She tore off one of the towels and patted her face with it. "I'm just glad you came out when you did."

"It's a good thing you don't live too far away." A flash of lightning lit up the evening sky. "Looks like we're about to get one heck of a summer storm."

She handed him her credit card. He ran it and handed her a receipt before heading toward the door. "I'll bring your car closer."

"Thanks, but that's okay." She smiled. "I'll just make a

mad dash for it."

"You sure?"

She nodded.

He handed her the keys and an umbrella. "We keep several of these on hand for customers. No need to get drenched if you don't need to. Besides, I'll never forgive myself if you came down with pneumonia."

She grabbed the umbrella. "Thanks for getting to my car so fast. I can tell by the parking lot that you guys have been busy."

"Not a problem." He smiled and opened the door for her. "Be careful going home."

She nodded and dashed across the lot. The wind threatened to rip the umbrella from her hand. When she reached her car, she yanked open the door, slid inside, and tossed the umbrella onto the back seat.

She sighed when she pulled into her driveway. She'd left the garage door opener inside on the kitchen counter. It would take at least a minute to run along the cobblestone pathway to her front door. Lightning streaked through the sky. She put the car in park and glanced in the back seat. She didn't feel like fussing with the umbrella again and she didn't want to call Philip to ask him to bring her one, either. If he was on a work call, she didn't want to bother him.

Her raincoat.

He'd purchased her a shiny, bright yellow one with a hood years ago, and it was in the trunk.

She got out of the car and closed the door before hitting the button on the remote to open the trunk. It popped open. She leaned in to get her raincoat and screamed.

Mr. Hale.

He looked like someone had beaten him to a pulp and stuffed him in her trunk.

She reached for his wrist. He had a pulse, but it was faint and fading.

She pulled her phone from her pocket. She needed to call 911. He needed help fast.

The phone rang in her hand. She didn't recognize the number and hit the end-call button.

Philip ran toward her. "Eve, why are you standing out here in the rain?"

She pointed to Mr. Hale. Philip gasped and took a step back. "What in the world?"

"I don't know, but he has a pulse. I'm calling 911."

Her phone rang again. She answered. "I can't talk now, I have an—"

A sinister laugh echoed across the line and into her ear. She quickly hit the speaker button.

"Hello there, Philip. I'm glad your wife put the phone on speaker because this message is for you. Tell the authorities that you lied and there's no need to investigate your father any further. Your wife's friend was just a warning. Next time, the body in the trunk will be hers. The bullet in the back of her head will let you know that there'll be no need to check for a pulse."

The laugh echoed through the phone again, and Eve could've sworn the ground beneath her feet shook.

The call ended, and she looked at Philip, who'd slipped his arms under Mr. Hale. "Call 911. Hurry." He ran toward the house as another streak of lightning lit up the sky. "I need to get him out of this rain."

She dialed 911 and then prayed as she rushed after Philip. "Lord, I have no idea what's happening, but please don't let Mr. Hale die. Please."

Chapter 8

Philip laid Mr. Hale on their living room couch.

Eve paused her prayers for Mr. Hale and immediately dialed Dani, his daughter.

She explained what happened as Dani sobbed into the phone. Dani then said she was heading to St. Matthew's, which was forty-five minutes from her home. She hoped to be there when her dad arrived.

Eve sat next to Mr. Hale on the couch and held his hand. "Hold on, Mr. Hale." She sniffed and wiped at her eyes before continuing. "Please hold on. Help is on the way."

He moaned and squeezed her hand.

His grip was strong. *Thank You, Lord. Please continue to give him strength.*

The police arrived and asked her and Philip a ton of questions. Thunder clapped overhead as the paramedics screeched to a halt in front of their home. Seconds later, they burst through the door and worked quickly on Mr. Hale. They then loaded him onto a stretcher and carried him to the ambulance. Eve stood at the door and watched as they pulled away, sirens blaring.

An officer was bent over the trunk of her car. Rain pelted his rain jacket and plastic-covered hat. He gathered items from her trunk and placed them into a clear bag.

A hand touched her shoulder, and she jumped. It was Philip. "The officers are about to wrap up here."

They were? How long had she been standing at the door looking out? It didn't matter. She turned and snatched her purse off the foyer table. "Good. I'm going to the hospital. I'd like to be there when Dani arrives."

An officer stepped between them. "That's not a good idea."

"Why? We've already answered all your questions and you've taken my cell phone to track the call we received. Is there something else you need from us?"

"Not now, but we'd like for you to stay away from the hospital until Mr. Hale is stable and able to talk with us."

"What? He's my friend, and I've already contacted his daughter. She's distraught and I'd like to be there for them."

"Not until he tells us that you weren't involved in what happened."

Philip stepped in front of the officer. "What did you just say?"

The officer took a step back. "We have deputies talking with Abe Thomas and his employees right now." The officer stepped onto the porch as two more policemen passed between them and jogged to their vehicles. The officer in front of them, whose name plate read Sgt. Dodge, continued, "We have statements from the auto shop and from you and your wife. But we don't have one from Mr. Hale. Until we do, we'll need Mrs. Stockton to stay away from the hospital."

"Are you saying you think she had something to do with this?"

"I'm saying, we need Mr. Hale to tell us what happened."

"He was in pretty bad shape." Philip swallowed and lowered his tone. "What if he passes away before he's able to?"

Sgt. Dodge adjusted his hat. "We'll cross that bridge when we come to it."

When the sergeant got in his car, Philip slammed the door and locked it. He ran his fingers through his hair and shoved his hands into his jeans pockets. He stared at the cherry hardwood floor for several minutes before looking at her. "I'm sorry, Evie. I am so, so, sorry."

"Who was that man on the phone, Philip?"

"I don't know, but there's no doubt my father is behind whoever it was."

She gasped. "But why would your father want to hurt a harmless old man like Mr. Hale?"

"To get back at me."

"But Mr. Hale had nothing to do with any of that."

"Doesn't matter. All he needed to know was that Mr. Hale was a friend of yours. Whoever my father hired probably has been watching you and the café. Like the caller said, what happened to Mr. Hale was a message meant for me. They wanted *me* to know they can get to you or your friends anytime they want."

Eve squeezed her eyes shut as an image of Mabel, beaten and bruised, flashed before her, followed by an even more horrific picture of Priscilla and little Heidi. They often stopped by after closing to help Mabel lock up. She shuddered. Her employees. All of them were now in danger. She had to contact them. Let them know what was going on.

She rifled through her purse.

"What are you doing?"

"Looking for my phone. I have to call my employees. I'm shutting down the café for a while."

Philip tugged the purse from her hands. "The police have your phone, remember?"

"Right." How was she going to contact anyone without her phone?

"Where's your laptop? Is it in your office at the café?"

"No, it's upstairs."

"Do you have their information on there?"

She did. Her laptop automatically synched with her office computer daily. She could access her files from there.

She headed toward the steps, but Philip grabbed her arm. "Did you set the alarm at the café?"

"No, because Mabel was still there when I left. She would've set it though before leaving. I'll check when I get to my computer. If she didn't, I can do it from my laptop. I'll also be able to activate the cameras." She opened her hand. "I need your phone."

He handed it to her, and she quickly dialed Mabel's number. She'd called it enough times to know it by heart. Mabel picked up on the first ring.

Eve blew out a breath. "Oh, thank God, you're okay."

"Of course, I am." Mabel's response was more of a question than a statement.

"Where are you?"

"Got home a few minutes ago."

"Good. I'm closing the café for a while. Don't show up tomorrow morning."

"What?"

Eve shared everything that had happened, then added, "Until we find out more, I'm closing the café. I don't want anyone else to get hurt."

Mabel clicked her tongue. "The devil is busy."

A picture of Henderson Stockton with horns sprouting from the top of his head flashed in front of her. So did the memory of the voice she'd heard on the phone. The man's tone had been so … dark. There hadn't been the *tiniest* bit of sorrow for what he'd done to Mr. Hale. And his laugh. Eve shuddered. Several voices echoed through that one sinister laugh.

But one of the voices hadn't been laughing.

It had been wailing.

Mabel continued. "I'll let Priscilla and the other girls know what's going on."

"Thank you."

"And don't worry about contacting the rest of the staff. I have their numbers in my phone."

"Thank you. And please let them know that I have no idea when we'll reopen. But they will be paid as if we never closed. Nothing changes. Not in their pay or their benefits."

"That's generous."

"It's not their fault that this has happened, and I don't want to disrupt their lives any more than I have to."

"I'll let them know."

"Oh, and Mabel? Did you set the alarm when you left?"

"Why? You're not planning on going back there are you?"

"No, but I can activate it from my computer if it hasn't been set. I don't want anyone trying to break in while it's vacant."

"I set it."

"Thanks. I'll call again when I know more."

"I'll be praying."

"Please do."

Eve clicked off the phone and handed it back to Philip.

It rang in his hand.

He stared at the phone. "It's my father."

She sucked in a breath. "Should we answer it?"

His lips tightened, and he placed the phone on speaker. "I ask for an investigation into my mother's murder and you go after *my wife's friends?*" His face reddened, and his temple pulsed.

"You told the police you're innocent. Part of me wanted to believe that you were. And now you pull a stunt like this?"

"Son, this is what I was trying to warn you about. Word of the investigation has awakened entities that should've been left sleeping. You have *no* idea what you've done. If only you'd given me a heads up—"

"So that you could've gotten rid of the evidence?"

"So that I could've made preparations to protect you and Eve."

"You're threatening us?"

"I had nothing to do with what happened to Mr. Hale. Everything is out of my hands now. Someone else is handling things. He's called in people you don't even want to know about. People who your grandfather and I knew all too well. People I've spent my life trying to shelter you from." He sighed heavily. "People your mother came within hours of exposing. She'd wanted to protect you, too."

"So why did you kill her?"

"Tomorrow morning, you're going to wake up to the news that I've left the country. It's true. It's only a matter of time before the investigation opens a Pandora's box that can't be closed."

"Where are you?"

"Can't tell you that, son. But I'm calling to let you know that you and Eve should do the same."

"What? You're telling us to leave the country?"

"Go anywhere you want. But your home is not safe. Neither are your businesses."

"Safe from what?"

"These people will do anything to halt this investigation. Even if that means killing you or your wife."

"Dad—"

"I tried to stop all of this, son. I really did. That's why I'm on the run." Henderson's voice lowered. "Killing you or Eve is the last thing they want to do. It'll shift the investigation into high gear. They don't want that, but they'll do it if necessary. Asking the police to stop the investigation at this point won't matter. They think you know more than you do."

"I don't know anything."

"*I* know that, but they don't. The two of you need to go into hiding. The longer you stay in Habakkuk, the more your loved ones are in danger."

"We're not going anywhere."

"Mr. Hale was a soft target. Easy to get to, easy to harm. But they have a list. Before they try to kill you, they're going to make you *wish* you were dead."

Philip swallowed. "Who's next on the list?"

"I don't know. That's the God's honest truth."

He looked at Eve. "Maybe we can go to—"

"Stop." Henderson interrupted. "I don't want to know where you're going. If they ever find me, I'll be tortured into giving up your location. I can't tell what I don't know."

"Dad, who are these people? You've got to tell me. How am I supposed to—"

"The only reason you're still breathing is because you *don't* know who they are." Eve heard shuffling in the background before Henderson continued, "Listen to me, son. This is important. They may say that they want you to put a stop to the investigation, but that's a lie. They already have people working on that. What they want is *you*. Eve is disposable to them, but they're going to try to recruit you. If you join them, you'll live. If you don't, they're going to cut your throat just like they're planning on doing Eve's. My advice to you? Give them your throat. That'll be better than being under the control of evil for the rest of your life. Trust me. I know."

Eve placed a hand over her mouth.

Philip stared at the phone.

"Son, I've said too much, and I've talked too long. This may be the last time I ever talk to you, but I wanted you to be aware of what's going on and …" Henderson coughed and choked back a sob. "I was the one who killed your mother. I was given a choice. Either I do it, or they would. I had to do it, son. They would've tortured her mercilessly and let her die a slow and painful death. And they would've made you watch. You would've belonged to them after that. I had no choice." His voice shook. "Your grandfather and I didn't lie to you, son. Your mother did have a weak heart. It only took a few pills to make it stop beating. She knew what I had to do. She only asked that I never let those people get their hands on you. I told her I'd do whatever it took. She then died peacefully in my arms."

Tears ran down Philip's face. Eve took the phone from him. "Henderson, you can't share information like that with us and then disappear. You have to come back and tell the authorities what happened to your wife. When you tell them what you told us—"

"I'll be found hanging in my jail cell the next morning."

"The Habakkuk Police Department is not like that and you know it."

"They're not. But there are people already behind those bars who are."

"You can't abandon your son like this."

"The further away I am, the better off he is."

"Don't leave him like this. Please."

"Eve, my days are numbered. Have you not heard anything I've said?"

"Philip needs you."

He sighed. "Tell you what. Three years from now, have him go to Bora Bora."

"Bora Bora?"

"Yes. On this day, three years from now. Have him go to a hotel there called Island Flower and ask for a young woman named Kaloni. If I'm still alive, she'll know where to find me."

"Three years from now? Why three years?"

"That's the deadline."

"For what?"

"Philip, you still there?"

Philip cleared his throat. "I'm here."

"I love you, son."

The phone clicked off.

She handed the phone to Philip. "*Lord,*" she asked silently. "*What in the world are we going to do now?*"

Chapter 9

"Thanks for coming in." Sgt. Dodge rose from behind his desk and extended his hand to Philip. "We'll look further into what your father said. If we find out anything else, we'll let you know."

Philip stood and Eve did the same before looking into the Sergeant's eyes. "Have you had the chance to speak with Mr. Hale yet?"

The sergeant shoved his hands into his pockets. "We have a deputy stationed outside his hospital room, however, he hasn't regained consciousness."

"Is it okay if I talk to his daughter then? She must be going crazy worrying about her dad, and wondering where I am."

"She knows her father was found in the trunk of a car, but we haven't told her *whose* car he was in. However, to avoid any future legal complications, it's best not to speak to anyone in his family right now."

"Sergeant, she knows her father was found in my trunk. I called her right after I called 911."

He sighed heavily. "You didn't mention that earlier."

"I didn't think I'd have to."

He folded his arms across his chest. "I'll have an officer talk to her about that call. Hopefully, you'll be able to speak with Mr. Hale soon, but right now, our main concern is his safety and yours. We're bringing in extra officers to watch your home. But that's a temporary fix. As you know, we're a small force. And since Henderson didn't give up any names, we have no idea who we're supposed to be looking for."

Philip shook his head. "We tried to get names from him, but he said we'd be better off not knowing."

"Doesn't matter. They know you and until *we* know more, we have to talk about your safety."

"No need to bring in extra officers," Philip said. "I've hired a private security firm."

Sgt. Dodge hiked a brow. "I wouldn't recommend using any company that worked for your father."

"We're not. A firm was recommended to us by one of Eve's friends. They've never had any dealings with my dad or his political cronies."

"Is the firm from around here?"

"No."

"Is the friend?"

"He's not, but his wife is."

"Good. When do they start?"

"Ten tomorrow morning."

"I'll have a couple of deputies follow you home. Let them clear the house before you go in. After that, they'll stay until your security team arrives."

Philip wrapped an arm around Eve's waist and they exited the police station. When they reached their car, Eve paused.

Philip looked at her. "You okay?"

"No. I think I'm just now starting to process everything that's happened." Her mind replayed Henderson's words about their safety. Her heart rate sped up. *Lord, help me. I can't have a panic attack right now.*

Philip wrapped his arms around her. "It's okay, Evie. Everything's going to be okay."

"The car."

"What?"

"The car. Should we check the car before we get in?"

"We're at the police station. No one would mess with our car here."

She sucked in a deep breath but it hitched. Philip pulled her tighter and gently massaged her back. "We're going to get through this, I promise."

Her breathing calmed. When her heart rate returned to normal, she inhaled the night air. "Thank you."

He kissed her on the forehead.

A car door opening drew her attention. Two officers were getting into a squad car. "I think they're waiting on us."

Philip opened the passenger door. After she was seatbelted in, he dashed over to the driver's side.

When he started the car, Eve closed her eyes. It had been a long time since she'd had a panic attack. This one was mild. In the past, they'd left her feeling paralyzed. Not physically. Mentally. Her thoughts would slow down to the point where she wasn't able to think clearly. Sometimes her brain froze, and she'd forget to breathe. Then she'd pass out. Thankfully, when those episodes happened, she'd been around friends who knew her well enough to know that she was fine. Her mind just needed a break from being overwhelmed.

It had been a long time since something like that happened, but if she wasn't careful, it would rear its ugly head again.

She needed to stay calm and gather her thoughts. The situation she and Philip were in wasn't going to get better any time soon. She didn't need any distractions. She needed to be alert and aware.

After the phone call with Henderson, they decided running away wasn't going to solve their problem. Besides, if they didn't know who they were running from, how were they supposed to know where to go? Whoever was after them could be anywhere. They prayed and asked God for wisdom. After that, they headed to the police station.

The time from when she'd picked up her car from Abe's until now had gone by at warp speed. A lot had happened, but the weight of it hadn't hit her until a few minutes ago.

Mr. Hale had been beaten within an inch of his life.

He may never fully recover.

Or he could die.

The police still weren't sure she wasn't involved in what happened to him.

And at this point, she wasn't sure that his daughter was either.

Her friends' lives had been threatened.

So had hers.

Her father-in-law had confessed to killing his wife.

She looked over at Philip. His face was set like stone, but she knew he was still reeling from everything he'd heard from his father.

And the realization that his mother had sacrificed her life for him.

Eve blinked away tears. She needed to focus.

On the way to the station, she'd called her friends and told them what Henderson had said. She wanted them to stay safe.

Kite and Jack Eagle had battled through their own life-threatening situations not too long ago and were already well-prepared security-wise. The same went for Barry and Priscilla King.

Lydia and her new husband, Steady, promised to upgrade their security setup right away. However, they were more concerned about Dinah's safety than theirs. She assured them that Philip hadn't mentioned to anyone, let alone Henderson, that Dinah was his daughter.

Mary hired a security team for her parents and siblings. A team they were already familiar with since Mary's husband, Ethan, and her adopted Dad, Ezra, had used them while conducting business deals between the States and Israel.

The team they used was part of a larger firm whose headquarters was in Tel Aviv, but they also had three smaller branches in the States. One on each coast and one in the Midwest.

Ethan recommended them to Philip, who then contacted them right away.

And tomorrow morning, three people from the firm's Midwest team would be living in her home. A man, a woman, and a K9 named Samuel.

Chapter 10

Eve brushed her hair, twisted it, and pinned the light brown curls to the top of her head.

The doorbell rang. She looked at her watch. Nine forty-five. The new security team wasn't due to arrive until ten.

Outside of her bedroom window, a black SUV with tinted windows sat in her driveway. A man, who was a foot taller than the deputy who watched their home overnight, stood talking with the officer. Next to him was a dog. The animal sat quietly next to him and appeared to be listening to the men's conversation.

Eve smiled. That must be Samuel.

She loved dogs, but when they'd agreed to have the K9 as part of their security detail, they'd been warned that they wouldn't be able to touch the animal. No petting, scratching behind the ears, rubbing their coat. Nothing. The man they'd spoken to yesterday had emphasized that Samuel was a highly trained K9 and was not to be treated like a pet.

Samuel had the features of a German Shepherd, but not completely. A mixed breed of some sort perhaps? She wasn't sure, but his coat sported various shades of brown and specks of black.

No matter the breed, he was cute as a button. She fought

the urge to run outside and play with him. Would she be able to restrain herself when he was living inside of her house?

The doorbell rang again.

She hurried down the stairs to open the door, but Philip beat her to it. A tall woman, taller than Philip, stood in the foyer. She was around six foot three, with long dark hair that was pulled into a tight bun at the nape of her neck. She had on a fitted black top with long sleeves and black pants. A handgun was attached to her belt, along with several other items Eve didn't recognize. She also carried a black leather case.

Philip turned to Eve. "Honey, this is Gila. She's part of our new security team."

Gila smiled and reached for Eve's hand. "We arrived sooner than we expected. I hope that's okay."

Eve shook her hand. "Not a problem. We're just glad you're here."

Gila motioned behind her. "My partner is talking with the police outside. He'll join us shortly. Along with our K9, Samuel."

"Yes, I saw them from my bedroom window." Eve looked around the foyer. "Are the two of you still planning on staying for a while? I don't see any luggage."

Gila nodded. "We travel light, but we do have a few items in the car. Before we bring them in, I'd like to have a look around your home if you don't mind."

"Not at all. I can show you around if you like."

"I'll be assessing potential security issues, so that won't be necessary. Eitan, my partner, and Samuel will check the outside perimeter."

"I see."

Gila stepped into the hallway and pointed to her right. "Okay, if I start with the rooms down this hall?"

"Sure. You'll come across a half-bath, a laundry room, and two bedrooms. Oh, and a couple of linen closets."

Gila nodded.

When she disappeared down the hall, Philip pulled Eve closer to him. "How are you doing?"

"I'm okay. It's still hard to believe that bodyguards will now be a part of our reality. However, everything that has happened over the past twenty-four hours has started to sink in."

"I know." He blew out a breath. "Last night I dreamed about my mom. We were walking hand-in-hand on my grandfather's old farm. I asked her a bunch of questions, but she didn't answer any of them. She just smiled."

"Sounds like a nice dream. How did you feel when you woke up from it?"

"I didn't think much about it at the time," he stroked his chin. "But I guess I felt … peaceful?"

"That makes sense. And it's probably because you're no longer wondering what happened to her."

"Yeah." He inhaled a deep breath and his shoulders dropped. "I also feel like a huge weight has been lifted off of me."

"You've been struggling a long time. Walking the line between loyalty to your father and the love of your mother couldn't have been easy."

"It was horrible."

She smiled. "Well, at least that part is over."

He shifted his gaze to the glass storm door. Eitan and Samuel walked the outline of their yard. Philip pointed to them. "But now, this." He turned to Eve. "Day by day, right?"

"Oh, no. A whole day is too much for me to take on right now. How about hour by hour?"

He chuckled. "Agreed."

Gila joined them again. The black leather case she carried was now strapped across her back. She held a clipboard with a pen attached to it in her hand. "I've taken notes on a few things that need to be secured. Both of the guest bedrooms have weak spots and so does the basement. I'll check the kitchen and the great room later. Right now I'd like to check upstairs. That includes the attic too if I can access it from up there."

Philip nodded. "There's a ladder, but be careful when you pull the latch. A spring broke on it a while ago and I haven't gotten around to fixing it. It'll come down hard if you pull it too fast."

She wrote something on her clipboard before heading up the stairs.

Eve walked into the kitchen. "Are you hungry?"

Philip rubbed his stomach. "Yeah."

"I am too." She placed a skillet on the stove. "I'll start breakfast."

"Or you could warm up the lasagna we didn't get to eat last night."

It was too early for that many carbs, but she really didn't feel like cooking. She was also starving. Microwaving a couple of plates of lasagna would be quick and easy. Since Philip made it, she doubted the meal would be enjoyable, but it would provide sustenance. The last thing she remembered eating was a couple of crackers and chicken salad. She had no idea when Philip had last eaten anything.

She pulled the lasagna from the refrigerator and paused when there was a knock on the door. A quick peek revealed it was Eitan. He introduced himself to Philip, and they talked for a few minutes about Samuel. Most of it she'd heard yesterday when Philip had agreed over the phone to work with Magen Security Agency.

Gila came down the stairs, and Eve turned back to the counter. She pulled four plates from the cabinet. She had no idea if Gila and her partner would be open to eating lasagna so early in the morning, but she wanted to offer it just in case.

Philip sat at the kitchen table, and Gila and Eitan joined him.

"Honey, " Philip called to her. " Gila and Eitan would like to talk to us about a few things."

"Sure." She switched on the coffee pot. "Would anyone like a cup of coffee? Or tea?"

They shook their heads.

"Lasagna?"

Gila hiked her brow, and Eitan smiled, but somehow she got the feeling that neither one of them was hungry.

She turned the coffee pot off and sat next to Philip at the table.

Gila spoke first. "Yesterday evening you spoke to Joseph, our boss and the head of our Midwest location. He briefed us on your file.

"Your situation is immediate and serious. However, the police have all of the files taken from your father's home, and his bank accounts have been frozen. We've been told it could take months before we're able to access that information. That slows us down in analyzing the threat. It also means that Eitan and I will need to be here longer than previously discussed with Joseph. The extra time and additional services could get expensive. Would you still like to proceed?"

"Yes." Philip crossed his arms over his chest. "Money's not an obstacle. I want you to do everything you can to keep my wife safe."

"Good." Eitan released Samuel's leash, and the dog lay down at his feet. "There are a few details we need to take care of first."

Gila wrote on a piece of paper clipped to her clipboard. "There are a couple of questions we have to ask."

Philip frowned. "Such as?"

"When was the last time the two of you had a physical?"

"A few months ago. Why?"

"Are you able to access the results?"

"Yes. We always print the reports after we've viewed them online. They're upstairs in my office. Do I need to go get them?"

She nodded.

He jogged up the stairs and quickly returned with the documents. Eitan opened the folder and read them. He pointed to something on one of the pages, and Gila glanced at it before looking at Philip. "You have a sulfa allergy?"

"Yes."

She made a note of it and continued reading through their records as Eitan flipped through the pages. "Any other drug allergies?"

Philip shook his head.

"What about food?"

"None."

Gila frowned. "Eve, there's not much in this folder about you."

"I've been blessed with good health."

"You've lost quite a bit of weight over the past year. Were you ill?

"No, but it was time to get rid of those extra fifty pounds." It had been, but she left out the part about how Philip used to call her a fat cow. She'd tried for years to shed the extra weight and failed. Until last year. She didn't know why, but something in her body changed, and the pounds slowly dropped off by themselves. Her doctor said it may have had something to do with changes in her metabolism. She didn't care what caused the weight loss but she was determined to maintain it. Her physician had stated in her medical file that her current weight was perfect for her age and height.

However, the familiar fingers of shame pulled on her. She closed her eyes. Wallowing in past hurts and self-pity wasn't going to get her anywhere. She silently thanked God that she had been able to lose the weight and keep it off. She also thanked Him for the Philip sitting next to her today. He'd matured significantly from the man he was just a few short years ago.

Gila continued. "Your physicals look good. I've also made note of your blood types. However, we like to keep a backup supply on hand. We have everything we need to do that in our vehicles. Would you be opposed to having your blood drawn by us?"

Eve shook her head. "Not at all, but why would you need to?"

"Because sometimes bad things happen. For example, a sniper on a rooftop. And as your Personal Protection Agents, or PPAs, we'll be the first ones responding to any injuries or medical emergencies. When seconds matter, having a backup supply of your blood type could save your life."

"Oh." Why was her voice shaking?

Gila leaned close and whispered, "It's okay. We can do that part later if you like. I know what we're saying right now is a lot to take in."

She had no idea. Eve fought to erase an image of Philip lying on the ground in a pool of blood, a bullet hole in his heart. The same heart he'd finally allowed God to minister to. A heart that only recently turned tender toward her. She nodded. "Later will be better. Thank you."

Gila tugged two sheets of paper from the clipboard and slid them across the table to Eve and Philip. "A list of your emergency contacts, please."

Eve reached for one of the pens Gila offered. Her hand shook. She clenched it into a fist until it stopped. She then grabbed the pen and quickly wrote down the contact information for her mother and Lydia.

Philip took the other pen and stared at the paper. Like her, Philip had no siblings, and the two of them didn't have any children. In the past, he'd always used his father as his emergency contact. But neither one of them knew where Henderson was. And he'd probably already tossed his old phone.

She placed a hand on Philip's arm. "I think you should put Pastor Greene down as your emergency contact, and your friend Harold."

He was about to jot the names on the paper when he spun in his chair toward her. "What about my daughter?"

Gila straightened, and Eitan slapped his hand down on top of the sheet of paper. "You have a *daughter?*"

Eve quickly explained about Dinah, but Eitan shook his head. "Even though she doesn't acknowledge Philip as her father and only a handful of people know, we still should've been notified of this in the beginning. We can't assume that word hasn't spread or that someone hasn't put two and two together. She needs protection ASAP."

"On it." Gila rose from her chair and snatched a phone from her belt before walking outside.

Philip wrote down the three names and shoved them toward Eitan. Eve knew her husband's aggression was because of the harsh tone Eitan had taken with him. Philip once again folded his arms across his chest. "Is there anything else?"

"Yes," Eitan replied. "According to our files, you've lived in this neighborhood for over thirty years. How well do you know your neighbors?"

"Well enough I guess." Philip shrugged. "There are only five homes on this stretch of road. Each one sits on two acres. Our neighbors down the road we know pretty well. The elderly couple across the street moved in about a year ago. Don't know them at all. Unfriendly type that keeps to themselves."

"Do you know their names?"

"Only that their mailbox says Smith."

Eitan frowned and reached for Gila's clipboard. He made a note of something and then put it back down. "Someone on our team will check them out. Are either of you active online? Any social media presence?"

"No."

"Good, but we will need the passwords to all your email accounts."

"No problem."

Gila quickly took her seat again. "We've contacted your daughter. We have someone on their way out to her now."

Philp bowed his head.

Eitan continued. "Samuel and I completed our threat assessment of the outside. I went ahead and secured some of the weak areas. Gila and I will work on the inside tonight. Until we know the exact nature of the threat against you, I recommend that the two of you not sleep in the same room until we do. Samuel and I will sleep in one of the bedrooms on this floor. Mr. Stockton, I advise you to sleep in the room next to me."

"No."

"Mr. Stockton—"

"I'm staying with my wife."

"She's not going anywhere. She's still going to sleep in the master bedroom, and Gila will be right outside her door. Your second-floor windows are high enough off the ground that no one will be able to climb up to them without our security system alerting us first. If someone tries to enter through one of the entrances down here, Samuel and I will stop them before they even reach the stairs."

Before Philip could protest, Eve turned to him. "Love, I don't want to be away from you either, but this is why we hired them, right? They're the professionals. We need to trust them."

Eitan added, "You'll always be able to have eyes on her. Cameras and monitors are going to be placed in all of the bedrooms. "You'll be able to see and talk to her all night if you'd like."

Philip raked his fingers through his hair. "Fine. Anything else?"

Eitan nodded. "When we're communicating via any electronic device, Eve will be referred to as Buttons and your code name will be Badger."

"Code names?"

"They're for safety reasons."

"Got it."

Eitan stood, and so did Samuel. "It sounds like a lot, but once Gila and I secure the inside of your home and vehicles, the four of us should be able to quickly establish a routine. Our goal is for you to be able to live as normal a life as possible. We'll be here protecting you 24/7, but we aim to have as minimal of an intrusion into your daily lives as possible."

"Thank you."

"We need to see your phones."

"The Habakkuk police still have Eve's phone."

Eitan looked at Eve. "Would you happen to have another one?"

She nodded and rummaged through the kitchen drawers until she found the small bin she and Philip tossed old and broken devices into.

She quickly reactivated the previous one she had before her last upgrade. It wasn't as fancy as the one the police had, but it still worked.

She handed the phone to Gila and Philip handed his to Eitan. The agents attached small wires to each device and pressed a bunch of buttons. After a few minutes, Eitan removed the wires and gave them back their phones. "To reach us, press and hold the number one."

They nodded.

Eitan motioned toward the front door. "Our SUV's are outside. We're gonna bring in some equipment and install it. Were the two of you planning on going anywhere today?"

Eve sighed. "No. We're staying here until we know more about what's going on and who's after us."

"Understandable, but that's not sustainable long term. You both have jobs right?"

"I own a café, but I've closed it temporarily."

"I'm working from home," Philip added. "Next week I'm scheduled to meet with a client in Kansas. I'll have my secretary reschedule that. My employees are aware of what's been going on with my father. There's been nonstop news coverage of him ever since he fled the country."

"Do they know about the threat to your lives?"

"No."

"Good. The less they know the better. However, restricting daily activities too much can become an issue. Mentally and strategically. If the two of you want to go somewhere, let us know ahead of time, and we'll make it happen."

"Thank you."

Eitan removed Samuel's leash. "Samuel's going to stay here with you while we gather equipment. He understands basic commands such as sit and heel, but for the most part, he'll sit quietly until I return. He's been fed, so he doesn't need to eat. And please, no treats."

When Gila and Eitan left, Samuel looked at Eve. His eyes bored into hers as though he was reading her thoughts. He then shifted his gaze to Philip and his eyes narrowed. He didn't growl or bark, but there was no mistaking the look on his face.

Philip chuckled. "I don't think he likes me."

Eve giggled. "I don't think he does either. He's definitely not a fan."

Philip walked into the great room and stopped in front of one of the windows. Samuel followed. The afternoon sun blazed through the panes and highlighted a huge spot on the cherry wood floor. Philip pointed to the circle of sunshine. "Sit."

Samuel sat. The sun's rays glistened against his already gleaming coat.

Philip smiled. "I think once we get to know each other, he'll become a fan."

"I don't know. I think he knows that you've broken my heart a time or two."

"What makes you say that?"

"Just kinda have a feeling."

"Oh, really?"

"Dogs are known to have the ability to pick up on all sorts of things."

"Yeah?" He walked over to her. "Let's see if he picks up on this." He pulled her tight against him and twirled a strand of her hair around his finger before placing it behind her ear. He gathered the rest of the hair in his hand and nibbled on her neck.

"Philip." Her body arched toward him. His arm tightened around her waist.

"Philip," she tried again. "I don't think we should be doing this in front of the dog." The words came out faster than she'd wanted them to. But she had no choice. Each kiss on her neck made it harder for her to breathe.

Without looking up, Philip asked, "Why? What is he doing?"

"He's looking at us."

"Ah," he chuckled in her ear. "Then let's give him something to look at."

He ran a hand down her back. Eve moaned.

The door opened and Eve whipped around toward it. Gila

stood in front of her.

"I was just bringing in some of the security equipment." Gila's cheeks reddened. "But that's okay, we can use the basement entrance, I'll just need the key to unlock it."

Heat flooded Eve's face. Why did she feel like she'd just been caught with her hand in the cookie jar?

Philip broke the silence. "I'll get the key for you."

He stepped away, and Gila smiled at her. "As Eitan said earlier, we don't want to disrupt your lives any more than we have to. If you'd like an hour or two alone with your husband, go for it. Eitan and I are here, and we'll keep an eye on things. But you'll have to take your phones with you and keep them on."

"We'll do that, thank you." Eve shook her head. "I don't know what happened, we just kind of—"

"No need to explain. Philip's your husband and the two of you are under a lot of stress. We all have different ways of dealing with it."

Was that what they were about to do? Relieve … stress?

Probably. More than likely.

Either way, she didn't care. Her body still tingled from Philip's kisses, and she'd just been given the green light by her PPA to spend a few hours alone with him.

She winked at Gila and walked toward the stairs. "See you in a couple of hours."

Chapter 11

Samuel barked.

Eve's eyes popped open. The sound was loud and sharp, but not close. She held her breath and listened.

Nothing.

She tossed off the sheet and swung her legs over the bed. The monitor Gila and Eitan had installed in their master bedroom showed views of each room of the house in full color. The time in the upper right-hand corner showed a quarter to seven.

Philip had left their bedroom late yesterday evening to settle in the guest bedroom downstairs. She looked for the guest room blocks on the monitor. She had a full view of the room Philip had been assigned to, but the view in Eitan's room only showed the door, and it was wide open.

Philip's room was empty.

It made sense that Eitan wouldn't be in his room, but where in the world was Philip?

She stood and reached for her bathrobe. There was a soft knock on the door before it opened. Gila stood on the other side.

"Morning, Eve. I saw on the monitor that you were awake."

"Philip isn't in his room. What's going on?"

"We had an unexpected visitor this morning."

Eve gasped.

"No need to worry. The situation is under control."

Eve tightened the belt on her robe. "Under control? A stranger came to my home, and you didn't wake me up to tell me?"

"The visitor isn't a stranger. He's someone you know. Your husband's on the front porch talking to him now. Philip asked me not to disturb you."

Someone she knew? A man? The only man she knew who would stop by their home this early in the morning was Roger. He'd done it many times to drop off songs for her to look over before he headed to the studio. But it couldn't be Roger. They told all their friends to stay away until this whole thing blew over. Besides, she and Roger had agreed to work virtually and had a meeting set up for later this morning. There was no need for him to stop by.

And apparently, Gila wasn't going to offer any further information. However, she did motion toward the monitor.

Eve glanced at the screens again. Philip was back inside the house and sitting in the brown leather chair next to the fireplace in the great room. Sitting across from him in the matching chair was …

No. It couldn't be.

Eve leaned closer to the monitor to get a better look, then turned to Gila. "That can't be who I think it is."

"He showed up this morning with the Sheriff. And he's not alone. He brought someone with him."

What in the world?

Eve searched the rooms again but didn't see anyone. "Who did he bring?"

"You should probably join them and let Philip fill you in."

"Give me five minutes."

Gila nodded and closed the door behind her.

Eve untied her robe and threw it across the bed. She

yanked off her gown and tossed it next to the robe.

She went to her closet and slid on a pair of jeans. Not her favorite style of pants, but she kept this particular pair nearby because they were comfortable and easy to slide into. She pulled on the sweatshirt lying next to them. She purchased the fall-themed sweatshirt last winter when it was on sale. Autumn was still a couple of weeks away, and the material was too heavy for the August heat, but like the jeans, it was easy to slip into. She needed to get downstairs as fast as possible and talk with her husband.

And her father-in-law.

What in the world could've brought Henderson Stockton back to Habakkuk? To his son's home? A son he'd warned he needed to stay away from for his own protection?

Had the Habakkuk police located him?

Had he been brought back to the States by the FBI?

Couldn't be. If that was the case they'd still have him in their custody.

She turned on the faucet, splashed cold water on her face, and dried it quickly with a towel.

Her hair was in desperate need of a brush, but it would have to wait.

She needed to get downstairs.

She needed answers.

She threw open the bedroom door and followed Gila to the great room. Philip waved her over to him. He kissed her on the lips, then made room for her on the overstuffed leather chair.

She studied his face. His expression wasn't one of anger, sadness, or hurt. He looked confused.

She glared at Henderson before turning her attention back to Philip.

He wrapped an arm around her. "Dad's been catching me up on some things."

"Like what?" She whipped her head in Henderson's direction. "And why are you here?"

"I'm here because of you."

"What?"

He placed his elbows on his knees. "The last time we talked, you said it would be wrong to abandon my son at a time like this." He scrubbed a hand over an unshaven face. "I couldn't get what you said out of my mind, so I did as you suggested. I contacted my lawyer, and he contacted the authorities. My life is still in danger, so the FBI agreed to meet us at a secret location."

"You turned yourself in?"

"Yes."

"Then how are you here?"

"Because I have information they want. When I leave here, I'll be taken to the same safe house they have Kaloni at."

"Kaloni?" Philip leaned forward. "The woman you told me to look for in Bora Bora three years from now?"

Henderson nodded. "The deal my lawyer negotiated with the FBI included bringing Kaloni to the States. That was non-negotiable."

Eve tsked. "Are you serious? You turned our lives upside down, and all you could think about was bringing your girlfriend here?"

"Kaloni isn't my girlfriend." He looked at Philip. "She's your sister."

Philip's head jerked back. "What?"

"Twenty-five years ago, when I was traveling, I met someone. We fell in love and shortly thereafter, got married. Kaloni was born that same year."

Eve couldn't believe what she was hearing. Philip's mother had died long before that, so Henderson hadn't cheated on her. But how was it possible that both Philip and his father had daughters the other didn't know about?

Philip's face reddened. "You got married twenty-five years ago and never told me? Never thought to mention that I had a sister?"

"I thought about it many times, son, but I couldn't. Knowing what I did to your mother … anyway, at the time, it just seemed easier to keep that part of my life separate from the one I lived here."

Philip stood. "Get out of my house."

"Son, try to understand, I—"

"Where's her mother? Did you kill her, too?"

Gila and Eitan, quietly listening from the kitchen table, turned their heads toward them. Samuel did, too, and Eve could've sworn he was inwardly growling at Henderson.

"I did not." Henderson looked up at Philip. "She died of breast cancer two years ago."

Philip shook his head and paced back and forth in front of their chair.

"Son, this is not how I wanted you to find out. Hopefully, we'll be able to discuss this more soon. I only have a few minutes before the FBI takes me to who knows where. They're outside waiting for your agents to escort me out. Will you at least look at me?"

Philip crossed his arms and stopped pacing, but stared at the floor.

"Fine." Henderson bowed his head. "I'll say what I've come to say and leave." He lifted his head again. "The group that's after us doesn't have a name. Me and a few others refer to them as *The Shadows*, because that's what they are. They're dark beings, with no names, that lurk behind everything we do. Especially, the political decisions we make.

"*The Shadows* have an endless supply of money. No one knows where it comes from, but the group has been around for decades. Your great-grandfather was the first one in our family to get involved with them. They gave him tons of money to do their political bidding and other nefarious deeds. When he died, your grandfather took his place.

That's why we're in the situation we're in now. No one knows the names of the people in *The Shadows*, but I do know the names of the people they've paid off. Part of my deal with the FBI was for me to share everything I knew about those people and their crimes. And I did that. But there's one name I need *you* to be aware of. He goes by the name G. Some say it's short for Garringer. He's not a member of *The Shadows*, but rumors suggest he's the grandson of one of them. He runs an offshoot of *The Shadows*, called *Legion,* and they've been spotted here in Habakkuk. There's no doubt in my mind that G and *Legion* are the ones they're going to send after you and Eve."

G. Where had she heard that name from?

Gila pulled a phone from her belt and whispered into it before heading outside.

Henderson stood.

Eitan and Samuel watched him closely.

Philip resumed his pacing.

Henderson cleared his throat. "We'll talk more about Kaloni, son, I promise. But I wanted to warn you in person about G. He's evil. Be careful."

Philip continued pacing.

"And there's something else," he shoved his hands into the pockets of his navy blue slacks. "There's a good chance in the next few weeks that Kaloni and I will be placed in the Witness Protection Program."

Philip stilled.

"The contract *The Shadows* put on my life doesn't expire until three years from now. When the FBI starts investigating and arresting the people I've named, the price on my head will triple. The FBI thinks it'll be a good idea for you and Eve to join us."

Philip looked at his father.

"Just think about it, okay?" Henderson nodded toward the door. "I gotta go."

Philip didn't respond.

Eitan scooted his chair back. He and Samuel followed Henderson out the door.

Philip plopped into the chair his father had vacated. "I've had a sister for twenty-five years, and he's never said anything about it. How could he keep something like that from me?"

What Henderson did was horrible, and she wanted to comment further on that, but how could she? She'd known for *years* that Dinah was Philip's daughter and never said a word to him. The reasons were as different as night and day, but would

Philip see it that way?

No, he wouldn't. The two people he trusted the most in the world had kept important information from him. She didn't want to add to his pain by sounding hypocritical.

Besides, there was something else niggling in the back of her mind. She'd never heard the name Garringer before, but she had heard someone reference the name G. And for the life of her, she couldn't remember who.

Her phone rang. She'd placed it on the kitchen counter yesterday and forgotten about it.

When she picked it up, Lydia's name was on the screen. Thank heavens. If anyone would be able to help her remember where she'd heard the name G, it would be her best friend.

Chapter 12

Philip frowned. "What?"

Eve placed four mugs on the table. Gila and Eitan were still outside talking with the FBI agents about Henderson's statements, but she'd brewed a full pot of coffee, just in case.

"Neta. Remember her? That horrible woman who said awful things about Lydia a little over a year ago?

"I remember Neta." His brows furrowed. "But what has she got to do with—"

"Neta used to work for someone named G."

His eyes widened. "Are you sure?"

"Yes." Eve sat across from him. "The day before Neta died, she talked about someone named G to Lydia. Neta had been pretty cryptic about it, but Lydia definitely remembers her talking about him."

"What did Neta say?"

"Lydia couldn't remember the details, but she got the impression that he was a very dangerous man."

"Does Lydia think this G person killed Neta?"

"No. I mean, I don't think so. Allison, a friend of Lydia's, told us she overheard the doctors say Neta's heart had stopped beating, or something like that. Neta had been beaten up pretty badly, and she also suffered from multiple stab wounds. We all assumed that had something to do with her death, but now, I'm not so sure."

"Huh."

Philip's "huh" started her thoughts racing. *Was the man Neta mentioned the same one that had been sent to harm her and Philip? If so, what was Neta's connection to him?*

Did she die as a result of her injuries? Or did G send someone to the hospital to kill her?

Eve shivered.

Mr. Hale hadn't been stabbed, but just like Neta, someone had used him as a punching bag. The similarities were too similar to ignore.

Philip pulled one of the mugs closer to him. The coffee. She'd forgotten to pour it. She grabbed the carafe from the coffee pot and poured the thick Ethiopian brew into his mug.

She poured a smaller amount into hers. The caffeine would help her wake up, but too much of the umber java would make her jittery.

And her insides were already shaking. "If the two G's are the same, that means he's been here for over a year."

Philip sipped his coffee. "Or he's returned."

Eve stared at him. *Was Philip right? Had G been ordered to return? This time not for someone he knew, but for them?*

Or was it because Philip's father and grandfather had belonged to the ominous group, that they figured Philip belonged to them as well?

Sweat rolled down her forehead and onto her cheek. She wanted to wipe it away but she only had enough strength to hold the carafe.

Philip stood and placed the carafe on the table before using his thumb to wipe the stream of perspiration from her cheek. He pulled her close.

She sucked in a breath and held it until her heartbeat returned to normal. "I'm sorry this keeps happening. It sneaks up on me. The fear. I'm fine one minute, then suddenly everything that could go wrong hits me at once."

"Considering our situation, you're doing remarkably well. Hour by hour, remember? We'll keep taking it slow."

She nodded against his chest, then returned to her seat. Eitan and Gila walked into the kitchen. Eitan leaned against the wall, Samuel at his feet. Gila stood in front of the pantry door.

Eitan spoke first. "The FBI has taken your dad to the safe house."

"Thanks for letting us know, "Philip said. "My wife just found out some additional information."

Eve told them about her conversation with Lydia.

"Sgt. Dodge briefed us on that incident," Eitan replied. "The FBI also has a file on this G character. It's a thin one, but we were able to pull important information from it." He pulled out his phone. "Your father was right. G also goes by the name, Garringer. He was born in Oregon but frequents this area often. No one's been able to determine why. And so far, only one photo has successfully been taken of him."

Eitan turned his phone toward them and enlarged the photo.

Eve looked at it. The man in the picture was tall and on the slim side, with thick dark hair, most of which was covered by a black Fedora hat. The trenchcoat he wore was black, as well as the rest of his attire. The only thing that stood out was his eyes. They were bright green.

And cold.

And lifeless.

If the man in the photo hadn't been upright, she would've sworn the eyes belonged to a dead man.

"Do you recognize him? Eitan asked.

She didn't. And neither did Philip.

"Good." Eitan tapped the screen and the photo disappeared. "That means he hasn't tried to get close to you under false pretenses." He turned to Eve. "And you're sure he's never visited the café?"

"Positive. I would've remembered those eyes."

He slid the phone into one of the many pockets of his Army green pants. "What are your schedules like today?"

Philip shared how he needed to go upstairs to his office

and read through a corporate contract his secretary sent over.

"I have a virtual meeting with Roger, my music producer, in an hour."

Gila sat next to her and said, "Sgt. Dodge wanted me to let you know that Mr. Hale has regained consciousness."

"Oh, praise God." Relief flooded her veins. "He's going to be okay, right?"

"Looks that way. He's up and talking and has given a statement to the police. Sgt. Dodge said you can go see him."

Philip placed a hand on top of hers. "That's good news, honey. That means you've been ruled out as a suspect."

Gila agreed. "We can go now if you like."

"We?"

"If you go, I have to go."

"Oh. Right."

"We'll ride together in my SUV."

They'd have to. The Habakkuk Police Department hadn't returned her vehicle yet.

Philip smiled. "Go on, honey. Talking with Mr. Hale and his family will be good for you."

It would.

Maybe.

Would Mr. Hale be upset that he'd been targeted because of her?

Would his daughter?

What if they didn't want to talk to her? Not just today, but ever again?

But most importantly, what if visiting the hospital would do the Hale's more harm than good?

What if Mr. Hale wasn't out of danger?

Chapter 13

Gila opened the passenger door for Eve.

The shift in Gila's demeanor was palpable. Inside the home, Gila had been relaxed and even talkative, which Eve had learned Gila wasn't apt to do often. But from the moment they stepped outside, her posture had stiffened, and she'd stopped talking.

Gila's previous comment about a "sniper on the roof" buzzed through Eve's brain. She quickened her steps, wanting to get inside the SUV as soon as possible.

Gila caught up with her, gripped her elbow, and continued escorting her to it instead.

When they were both inside the vehicle, Gila turned to her. "I apologize for grabbing your arm. Did I hurt you?"

Eve shook her head.

"I should've mentioned that you're not to walk away from me. Ever. Even for something as simple as getting in and out of a car. Make sure I'm by your side before doing any of those things, okay?"

"I'm sorry, I wasn't thinking."

Gila smiled. "No apology needed. It takes some getting used to. But remember, when we get to the hospital, stay in the car until I open your door. A bit awkward I know, but it's for your safety and mine."

Eve nodded.

Eitan and Gila had turned their home into a fortress. The windows and doors had been fitted with devices that elicited ear-piercing shrills when anyone without a disarming code came within five feet of them.

A slew of cameras had been installed inside their home and out. Even the large sugar maples and rose bushes surrounding their house had miniature cameras and listening devices attached to some of their branches and stems.

But apparently, when they were out in the "wild" it was a different story.

Despite the information Henderson had shared, Eve had felt safe in her home. The security steps that had been taken as well as her being able to look at the monitors had given her a sense of security.

Unlike now, where she felt like a sitting duck.

Gila drove out of their neighborhood and made a right turn onto the main road. The five-mile stretch had deep woodlines on both sides and ended at Deer Pass, the only road near their home that led to the highway.

When Deer Pass came into view, Gila murmured something and tightened her grip on the steering wheel. Ahead of them at the intersection, was a black Econoline van blocking their path. Gila put the SUV in reverse. As they sped backward, she tapped her earpiece. "Code Orange." Eve reached for the grab handle as Gila mashed on the accelerator. They barreled backward until a second Econoline van, similar to the first, rushed toward them and turned sideways, blocking the road.

They were boxed in.

"Code Red," Gila shouted into the earpiece and snatched her firearm from her belt. The SUV lurched when Gila stomped on the brakes. Eve tightened her grip on the handle but Gila pushed her to the floor. "Get down."

Eve scrunched into a ball on the floor. When she heard Gila exit the vehicle and fire her weapon, she prayed. "Lord," her voice shook uncontrollably. "Please keep her safe!"

The passenger door yanked open, and Eve screamed. Gila pulled her from the vehicle and pushed her toward the woods.

Gila followed close behind her and continued firing her weapon. Four large men, all wearing ski masks and dressed in black, returned fire.

Pine needles and hickory leaves brushed across Eve's face and she lost sight of Gila. She bolted deeper into the woods, and tripped over a thick branch, her face smacking the rocky ground. More bullets. A lot of them. Where was Gila? Was she okay? She wiped dirt from her eyes and searched for her.

"Eve, over here."

She followed the whisper to a large oak a few feet away from her. Gila patted the ground. "Sit next to me."

Eve crouched behind the massive tree trunk. Gila pointed to her earpiece. "Waiting for the all clear."

All clear? The codes Gila called in earlier must've been for backup. That would explain the rapid gunfire. The guns the men from the van had shot at her and Gila with hadn't made any noise.

She leaned her head against the tree. What was happening? She sucked in a breath and released it in short, shaky spurts. She sucked in another one and realized the gunfire had stopped. She looked at Gila who was talking into her earpiece. She was talking softly but how could Eve not have heard it? Panic was setting in. She pushed away from the tree and looked at her hands. They were shaking. She pressed them against her face to steady them.

Gila tapped the earpiece. "We have an all-clear." She stood and reached for Eve's hand. Eve gasped. Gila's hand was covered in blood.

"You're hurt."

Gila looked at her left arm. "Bullets went clear through. I'm okay."

She'd been shot?

Eve scrambled off the ground. "We need to get you to a hospital."

"My brother's a trained medic. He'll take care of it."

"Your brother?"

"Eitan."

"Eitan's your brother?"

She winced. "Yes."

Eitan was her *brother*? When were they going to divulge that important piece of information? Eve shook off the annoyance. They could talk about that later. Right now, Gila needed help.

"Eitan's back at the house. I'm not waiting until we get back there. I'm calling 911 as soon as we get back to the main road."

"Eitan's already there waiting on us." Gila nudged her forward. "Let's go."

When they reached the road, Eitan ran toward them. What appeared to be an automatic rifle hung from his shoulder. He looked at Eve. "Did one of the men attack you?"

"No. Why?"

"Your face."

"What about it?"

"It's bruised and scratched."

It was? She closed her eyes and focused. Had she been attacked? Images of her jumping over rocks and fallen branches filled her mind. "No, I wasn't attacked. I tripped and fell."

"Did you lose consciousness?"

She had no idea, but she didn't want him focusing on her right now. She wanted him to tend to his sister, who miraculously was still able to stand next to her without any help. "I'm okay, but Gila's been—"

"Evie!"

Philip rushed toward her. "You're alive." He pulled her into a hug. "Thank You, God."

Alive? Had she been *that* close to death? A bullet whizzing past her head and lodging in the tree in front of her flashed before her eyes. Of course, she had. She sobbed into his chest. Minutes later, he handed her a tissue. She stepped back to blow her nose and screamed.

A man, wearing all black, lay in a pool of blood at Philip's feet. Another was a few feet away from him, on his back. Eyes open.

"It's okay, Evie. Eitan had to do it. When we pulled up, they started shooting at us." He paused and then added, "Eitan removed their masks and sent pictures of them to the FBI. There's a chance Dad might recognize them."

Her heart raced. How had her life come to this? Men shooting at her, men dying. She sucked in a breath and stared at the lifeless bodies. She longed to kneel next to them and pray for their souls, but what would be the point? It was too late. She hoped someone had shared the gospel with them before they died. But if someone had, would they have been shooting at her and Gila? The look on the man's face whose eyes were open reminded her of a horror film she'd seen as a child. His eyes were wide and his lips were parted in a way that made her wonder if he'd died mid-scream.

Or if he was screaming now.

For the rest of eternity.

She wiped away a tear. "There were four of them. Where are the other two?"

"One's in the back of Eitan's SUV. Wounded but alive. The other is on the ground behind the SUV. He had a faint pulse when Eitan ran to retrieve his medical bag. When he returned, it was too late."

Eve nodded and headed toward Eitan's SUV. Philip grabbed her arm. "Where are you going?"

"How bad is he?"

"Who?"

"They guy Eitan wounded."

"He's in pretty bad shape, but Eitan thinks he's going to make it."

"What if he's wrong?"

"Who, Eitan?"

She nodded. "What if the guy *doesn't* make it?"

"We already called the paramedics. Whether he lives or

dies is out of our hands.”

“But his soul isn’t.”

Philip stepped in front of her. “There’s no way I’m letting you go anywhere near that man, Evie. He tried to kill you.”

“I know, but—”

“But nothing. I know you want to share the Salvation message with him but now is not the time or place. For all we know, he has reinforcements on the way.”

“The police are on their way too, right?”

“As well as other Magen agents. They all should be arriving any minute now. Until then you’re staying close to me.” He tilted his head toward Eitan and Gila, who were now standing next to Gila’s SUV. Eitan motioned them over. “And both of us are going to stay close to them.”

“Did Eitan kill all three of those guys?”

“Yeah.”

“By himself? Or did you …?”

“I would’ve, but Eitan wouldn’t give me a weapon. Said he didn’t want to make me a target. So I prayed.”

She thought about the bullet that barreled past her head and smiled. “I’m glad you did.”

“I’ve never prayed so hard in my life. I don’t know what I’d do if anything happened to you, Evie.”

She blinked away tears. That simple sentence meant so much.

He pointed at Gila. “Is she okay?”

Gila was now on the ground next to her vehicle. Eitan sat beside her, pouring clear liquid onto a bandage.

“She was shot.”

“What?”

“She said she’s okay, that the bullets went clean through or something like that. By the way, did you know they were brother and sister?”

“No, but I can’t say I’m surprised.”

“Why?”

“On the paperwork we signed I noticed they had the same last name. They don’t act like they’re married, so I thought it was just a coincidence. However, Joseph, the head of Magen's Midwest Division, also has the same last name of Pearl. Now I'm guessing he's their dad."

"Oh."

Sirens wailed in the distance.

He grabbed her hand, and they walked slowly toward Eitan and Gila. "Before the police get here, tell me what happened. What do you remember?"

"There wasn't much to it and it all happened so fast. We were on our way to the hospital, heading toward the highway, when we were blocked in by two vans."

"Your face. Did one of them ..."

"No. We took cover in the woods." She touched her face. "This is just the result of me being clumsy."

He chuckled before turning serious again. "The paramedics will be here soon. I'd like for them to have a look at you."

"Yeah. The right side of my face hurts like crazy. I don't think I've broken anything, but I'd like to make sure."

The sound of rubber against the pavement caused her to turn around. A silver sedan approached. She recognized it. It was the Smiths, the neighbors that lived across the street from them.

Eitan stood and pointed his rifle at the car. Eve lifted a hand. "It's just our neighbors."

Gila pulled out her weapon and stood next to Eitan.

Philip tightened his grip on her hand and hurried to Gila's SUV. He yanked the door open. "Get in. Hurry."

Eve stepped inside. "Philip, what's going on?"

"I don't know. Let me find out."

She looked out the back window. Eitan was talking with the Smiths, but Gila's gun was still aimed at their sedan. Philip stood behind Gila.

Eve chewed her lip. She'd told Eitan that the Smiths were their neighbors, but he didn't lower his weapon. The Smiths were an elderly couple, maybe in their late seventies. They weren't a threat, but Gila and Eitan were sure treating them like they were.

Two police cars pulled up behind the Smiths, followed by an ambulance. Gila tucked her gun in her holster and went to talk with the police. Eitan joined her.

Several more police cars arrived. After what seemed like forever, Eitan jogged over to Philip and whispered something in his ear before turning to talk with two men who looked like FBI agents.

Philip ran toward the SUV she was in and opened the car door. "How's it going in here?"

"It'll go a lot better if you were in here with me."

He leaned in. "I know, but I get a better sense of what's going on by standing outside the vehicle."

"Okay." She swung her legs toward the door. "I'll join you."

"Please stay inside. The SUV is bulletproof."

"No one's going to try anything here. Police are everywhere."

"Don't fight me on this, Evie. Please don't. Do it for me, okay?"

The look in his eyes tore at her heart. Fear radiated from them. She hadn't thought about what he might've gone through when Gila sent out a Code Red. Did he cry out? Did he panic? Did he jump into action with Eitan? She had no idea, but one thing was clear. Whatever he did, he'd done it afraid.

Afraid that she might've been injured.

Or worse.

If she'd ever doubted his love for her—she didn't anymore.

The swarm of law enforcement on the scene would be a deterrent to anyone wanting to finish what the men in the Econoline vans started. She could step out of the armored enclosure and be safe.

That he didn't want her to defied logic.

She'd learned a long time ago that love defeated logic every time.

And if that meant staying put so her husband's mind

would be at ease .. then so be it.

Chapter 14

The curtain separating Eve from her would-be killer was thin.

She hadn't minded the paramedics looking over her injuries, but she had protested against being taken to St. Matthew's Hospital. Once they'd confirmed she hadn't broken anything, a couple of extra-strength aspirins would've been all she needed. However, they insisted she get imaging scans done to rule out internal bleeding, and Philip agreed.

The scans came back negative. She was fine.

The same couldn't be said for the man in the medical bay next to her.

She'd learned his name was Patrick Holman. She couldn't see him due to the curtain separating them, but she could hear what was being said.

While trying to disarm Eitan, he'd been shot in the abdomen, and the E.R. physician was letting him know he needed surgery. The doctor didn't sound hopeful, and neither did Patrick.

When the results of her scans came back, she'd been cleared to leave. Her physician went on to tend to another patient, and Philip was in the restroom a few feet away from her. She couldn't see them, but she knew hospital security, a

Habakkuk police officer, and Eitan and Gila were outside her curtained room as well.

When Patrick's doctor walked past her toward the exit, she grabbed her purse and quietly pulled the privacy curtain aside. She wanted to see the man who had wanted her dead.

His right hand and foot were cuffed to the bed rail, and he stared at the ceiling. He blinked and said, "Hi, Eve."

She inched closer. He had sandy-brown hair, gray eyes, a nose that spread wide across his face, and a goatee. "You know my name."

"I know all the names of the people I was hired to kill."

His voice was weak, and he grimaced when he talked. She needed to make this quick. "Live by the sword, die by the sword."

He chuckled, then coughed. "The irony."

"It's not funny. I heard what the doctor said. The chances of you surviving long enough to see the sunrise are slim. With or without surgery."

"I get it." He coughed again. "You're talking to a dead man."

"Dead to this world, yes. But it doesn't have to end there."

He turned his head toward her. "I tried to kill you."

"That doesn't matter much right now does it?"

"If you're offering prayer," he pressed his lips together and swallowed. "I'm all ears."

"I'll pray for you, but in case this is your last night on earth, I'd also like to talk to you about Jesus."

He stared at her and then closed his eyes. A tear ran down his left cheek. "I'm listening."

She held out her hand, and he placed his unshackled one in hers. She shared the message the Lord placed on her heart, and afterward, he agreed to confess his sins. His words were soft, but that didn't stop her from hearing the graphic details of the sins he'd committed. The ones she could tell were still heavy on his heart. He also repented of walking away from the Lord in his teens, asked for forgiveness, and acknowledged and accepted Christ as his Savior, all with little help from her.

Afterward, he shared how he knew this day would come and how he was sure it was his mother's prayers that had brought Eve to him in his darkest hour. He then asked if she would contact his mother if he didn't make it through surgery.

She agreed and retrieved a pen and a piece of paper from her purse, then wrote down the information he gave her.

The curtain behind her slid open. Two women stood there. One of them said they needed to prep him for surgery. Behind them, stood Philip and Sgt. Dodge.

Eve squeezed Patrick's hand. "Godspeed."

He nodded.

She let go of his hand and grabbed ahold of Philip's.

Sgt. Dodge followed close behind them as they made their way through the Emergency Department.

When they reached the parking lot, Sgt. Dodge turned to Eve. "What you did in there was not okay. That could've turned into a hostage situation real quick."

"He's dying, Sgt. Dodge. Hurting me was the last thing on his mind."

"It was dangerous and dumb."

"Hey." Philip stepped in front of her. "Enough."

Sgt. Dodge lowered his head. "In my line of work, you see a lot of good men get gunned down over the stupidest things. I'd be lying if I said their deaths haven't taken a toll on me. I just didn't want to see any of my men get hurt over something so preventable." He exhaled and stepped around Philip. "Nevertheless, what I said to you was highly unprofessional, Eve. I apologize."

"No apology necessary. My intention wasn't to put anyone's life in danger."

"I know." He looked over her head, and she turned. How long had Eitan and Gila been standing there?

He handed Eitan a folder.

Eitan flipped through it quickly, then said, "Thanks, Sergeant. We've got it from here."

Philip grabbed Eve's hand and followed behind Eitan and Gila. When they slid into the back of the SUV, he turned to her. "You're amazing, you know that?"

"What do you mean?"

"You had mercy on the man who tried to kill you. You prayed for him and helped lead him back to the Lord. I never would've done that. To be honest, I don't want him to be at peace with God. I want him to burn in hell for what he tried to do to you."

"I didn't think about it all. It just … happened."

"Well, I'm glad God chose you to do it and not me. Because babe, I'm telling you, I wouldn't have."

"You've come farther than you think, Philip."

"Not that far." He scooted closer and leaned her head on his shoulder. "That's why you're amazing. Even though you won't admit it, what you just did took a lot of guts. And faith. You always see the big picture and in this case," he kissed the top of her head. "You saw the eternal one."

She snuggled against him. Philip was angry at Patrick, but was she? Or had she been? She searched her heart. If she had any underlying anger and bitterness toward Patrick, she couldn't find it. Maybe she was too tired to be bitter. It had been a long day. All she'd wanted to do was go see Mr. Hale in the hospital. Well, she made it to the hospital, but she never got to see her friend. The Habakkuk Police and Eitan had said it was too dangerous, but they could've saved their breath. There was no way was she going anywhere near Mr. Hale or his daughter. They'd been harmed enough. Not by her but *because* of her.

She was angry at the men who beat up Mr. Hale, but she wasn't mad at Patrick and she wasn't sure why. Was it because those guys were still alive and well somewhere, possibly unleashing more harm on innocent people?

Maybe.

Patrick wasn't going to live to see tomorrow. She didn't know how she knew, but she did. So did he. He'd told her so. And undoubtedly, that was why he was so sincere in seeking the Lord.

While he could.

She glanced at the folded piece of notebook paper in her hand.

Nancy Holman was his mother's name. Once Eve was officially notified of Patrick's death, she'd call her. It was the last thing she wanted to do. There was no telling how his mother would respond. Would she sob uncontrollably? Or would she yell and scream at Eve?

She didn't know. Either way, it wouldn't change the miracle that had happened.

Another name had been written down in glory.

And his name was Patrick Holman.

Chapter 15

Eve sat at her writing desk and opened her laptop.

Philip walked into the bedroom and leaned against her desk. "Sgt. Dodge called. Mr. Hale was released from the hospital this morning. He's staying with his daughter and her family."

"I'm so glad. And I know Dani's happy he's back home with her."

"I asked Magen to provide security for them as well."

"Philip, there's no way they'll be able to afford that. Mr. Hale hasn't worked at the university in years, and Dani's a stay-at-home mom. Her husband works, but he's a—"

"It doesn't matter. I told the agency I'll pay for whatever they need."

She smiled. "Thank you."

"My family started this nightmare. It's the least I can do."

"Did Dodge say anything else?"

"Are you asking about Patrick Holman?"

"Yes."

His forehead wrinkled. "He didn't survive the surgery."

Eve nodded and opened her desk drawer. The piece of paper she'd tossed in the night before with Patrick's mother's information on it, stared up at her.

"Eitan was able to access his criminal record. He was a bad guy, Evie. He's been a hired assassin for a while. He's killed a lot of people. And those he didn't kill, he tortured."

"I know. He confessed a lot of those things last night. He knew his time was short."

"Do you think his deathbed conversion was real?"

"I do."

"Doesn't seem fair does it?"

"That a man who brought sorrow to so many, is now in the arms of Jesus?"

"Yeah."

"No, it doesn't. But it's consistent."

"With what?"

"The depth of our Father's love for us."

"Hmph." After a few seconds he added, "Are you getting ready to call his mother?"

She bit her lip. "Yeah."

"I can stay if you want me to. I haven't started working yet."

She'd love for Philip to hold her hand through what was sure to be a difficult conversation. But if the conversation went awry, he'd insist she'd end it, and she just didn't have the heart to do that to a grieving mother, no matter how she reacted.

"I appreciate the offer, but it's probably best that I do it alone. I'll text if I need you."

He nodded and closed the bedroom door softly behind him.

She glanced at the clock on her nightstand. Ten a.m. She didn't know what time zone his mother lived in, but even if she was an hour or two earlier, it'd still be daylight. No one liked receiving phone calls before sunrise.

She lifted her cell phone from the desk and dialed the number she'd scribbled down the night before. A woman answered after the third ring.

"Hello?"

"Mrs. Holman?"

The woman paused before answering, "This is Nancy.

Who's calling?"

"My name is Eve. I'm a ..." She was what? She wasn't a friend of her son. She wasn't even a member of the hospital staff or law enforcement. "I have news about your son, Patrick."

"He's dead, isn't he?"

How could she know that already? Had the hospital or police contacted her? No, they couldn't have. Otherwise, she wouldn't have asked the question. Eve swallowed. "Yes, ma'am. I'm afraid he is."

Soft sobs came through the phone line. After a few seconds, she asked, "Are you his wife? Girlfriend?"

"No. I just met him yesterday."

"Where?"

"St. Matthew's Hospital."

"The one in Habakkuk?"

"Yes. Are you familiar with it?"

"I was a nurse there. Decades ago. Are you an employee?"

"No. Patrick and I were in the E.R. together. That's how we got to know each other."

"Oh." Nancy sniffed. "Would you happen to know why he was in the E.R.?"

Eve thought about sharing the short version of the story. That Patrick had been shot, and that the two of them got to know each other while he waited to be wheeled into surgery. But somehow she didn't think Nancy would believe that's all there was to the story.

"I know the kind of life my son lived," Nancy added. "You can tell me."

Eve's stomach clenched, but if it had been her son, she would want to know the truth. All of it. The good and the bad.

She shared everything from Patrick trying to kill her and Gila to the last conversation she had with him before he headed to surgery.

Nancy listened quietly on the other end before saying, "I was on my knees all day yesterday for him. And late into the night, until I fell asleep on the floor next to my bed."

"He told me about your Christian faith and how you've prayed years for him."

"Yeah, but yesterday was different. I started off praying fervently for Patrick, but it was as if the Lord was more interested in ministering to me. Like he was preparing me for this conversation." She chuckled softly, then added, "Now that I think about it, that makes sense. He already knew how Patrick's story was going to end. I'd given up on praying for Patrick's lifestyle to change years ago and focused my prayers on him accepting Jesus again before he died. Little did I know, He'd already planned to put you in Patrick's path. You didn't have to do what you did, but I'm *so* glad you did. You were an answer to years of prayers. My heart can finally be at peace regarding Patrick. Thank you."

"It was all God."

"True. But you could've left that E.R. and never looked back. No one could've blamed you if you had. But instead, you allowed God to use you. I don't have the words to share how grateful I am."

As the conversation continued, Eve learned that Nancy hadn't seen her son in years. He'd said it was for her safety. Just like what Henderson had said to her and Philip. Nancy didn't know much about the people Patrick worked for, just that they were dangerous.

Nancy said she'd get a phone call from him twice a year, always from a different number. The last time she talked with him was on his birthday. He'd turned thirty-eight years old last spring.

Nancy lived in Arkansas and was already in her car, ready to make the three-hour drive to Habakkuk. She wanted to see her son one more time before making his final arrangements. She invited Eve to attend the services.

Eve declined. Not because she didn't want to go but because she was sure Philip would veto it. So would Eitan and Gila.

Nancy asked her to keep in touch, and she promised she would before they ended the call. She placed the phone back on her desk, and it trilled again. It was her mother. She tapped the call button.

"Hi, Mom."

"Sweetheart, what in the world is going on?"

"What do you mean?"

"I received a call this morning saying you had been in an accident or something."

"What?" She hadn't contacted anyone after she and Philip returned home last night. They'd fallen asleep in each other's arms on the couch. Philip would've told her if he'd called her Mom. So how did she hear about what happened?

"Who called?"

"Lottie."

"Who's Lottie?"

"Lottie Smith. Your neighbor across the street."

Why in the world would Mrs. Smith call her Mom? How did she even have her mother's phone number?

"Mom, is she a friend of yours?"

"Lottie? No. She said she just wanted me to know that she and her husband saw you and Philip yesterday. That you had been involved in an incident, and that there had been a large police presence. She thought you might've been injured."

"If you're not friends, how does she have your phone number?"

"Sweetie, I don't know, and I don't care. But I do want to know what's going on. Are you okay?"

"Yes, both Philip and I are fine."

Her mother let out a heavy sigh. "Thank God. I'll be there soon."

"Mom, things are a bit crazy here right now. I'd feel better knowing you were safely tucked away in Florida."

"Too late."

"What do you mean?"

"I'm no longer in Florida. I'm at Lambert."

Lambert Airport was in St. Louis. "Mom, you should've told me you were coming. I would've—"

"You would've what? Told me to stay *safely tucked away in*

Florida while someone's trying to kill you?"

"Lottie told you that?"

"No. I called Donna after Lottie called me. I begged and pleaded with her to tell me what was going on with you and Philip because I knew you wouldn't."

Donna Melson was her friend Mary's mother and Mom's best friend. Both were fully aware of everything that was going on because she'd updated them and her other friends regularly. She coveted their prayer support. However, she'd forgotten to tell them that she hadn't been updating her mother.

"Mom, I didn't want you to worry."

"I know, and I'm not mad. It was just upsetting to hear that you'd been injured in a phone call from a stranger."

"I'm sorry, Mom."

"And it was also upsetting that I was so far away. That's why I got on a plane immediately after talking to Donna. I wanted to be closer to you."

"Mom—"

"Don't worry. St. Louis is the closest I'm going to get for now. Donna thought it was odd that Lottie Smith would contact me when she's not a close friend of yours. She wanted to make sure I wasn't walking into a trap of some kind. That's why I took a plane here and not to an airport in the Ozarks."

St. Louis was five hours from Habakkuk, and Lambert was a huge international airport, unlike the smaller ones in the Ozark area which made it easier to spot someone.

"Where are you?"

"We're exiting the airport now."

"We?"

"Mary sent a security team to pick me up at the airport. I'll be staying with them at a hotel not too far from here. They asked that I give them my phone, and they're going to give me a new one. I'll call you from that one later, so you'll have the new number."

"Mom." Eve blinked away tears. "I hate that you're so close, and I can't come see you."

"Don't worry about it. I was going to fly closer to you

guys and have you and Philip pick me up, but when Donna told me that the Smiths had been questioned by your agents *and* the Habakkuk Police, we decided to be a bit more cautious until this all blows over." She chuckled. "At least we're in the same state now."

"I'm glad you reached out to Donna. And I'm sorry for how I reacted earlier. I really am glad you're here."

"I am, too. I'll call you later after I settle in."

"Love you."

"Love you, too. And Eve?"

"Yes?"

"Don't keep me out of the loop anymore. I don't know if I can take another heart-stopping phone call from a stranger telling me what's going on in your life. Trust me, my imagination is a whole lot worse than anything you could ever tell me. "

"I'll keep you updated from now on, Mom. I promise."

"Thank you. Talk to you soon."

Her mother ended the call, and Eve swiveled her office chair until it faced the bedroom window.

Only the roofline of the Smiths house was visible.

Who were they, really?

When the Smiths moved across from them two years ago, she and Philip had greeted them with a welcome basket. At least, they'd tried to. Mrs. Smith had opened the door, and she didn't look happy to see them. She didn't even say, hi. When they offered her the fruit basket, she refused to take it, saying her husband didn't like fruit.

She then closed the door. She didn't slam it, but they'd gotten the message.

Mr. and Mrs. Smith didn't want to be bothered.

Which made it all the more interesting that they seemed so concerned about her and Philip yesterday after they drove up to the scene.

Unbeknownst to Eve, the Magen Agency had done some digging on their neighbors. Turns out, the Smiths were from Oregon.

The same place G was from.

Which explained Eitan's and Gila's behavior when the Smiths showed up. Had they suspected the Smiths were involved with G? If they had, why hadn't they mentioned anything to her and Philip?

Eitan hadn't even let the Smiths leave until the police arrived.

At the time she thought it was a bit much considering all their neighbors had to take that same road to get to the highway. For all Eitan knew, the Smiths simply could've been on their way to the market.

But now that she thought about it, it was odd that they were the *only* ones to drive by so soon after the shootout.

And even odder that Lottie Smith had called Eve's mother.

Everyone in Habakkuk knew her mother. Kay had been born and raised here, and her phone number was the same as when she purchased her first cell phone twenty-five years ago. Almost everyone in town had it. It wouldn't have taken much for Lottie to get it.

But why go through all that to call someone you didn't even know? And whose daughter you'd barely spoken ten words to?

Was it to scare her mother so she'd fly back to Habakkuk?

If so, it worked.

Kind of.

Thankfully, her mother's and Donna Melson's discernment had warned her to stay away from Habakkuk.

But what had been the Smiths' plan? If they were associated with G and his people, what were they going to do? Were they going to meet her mother at the local airport? Saying that Eve and Philip had sent them?

Then what?

Would they have kidnapped her? Threatened her? Harmed her?

A chill went down Eve's spine. Henderson had said *The Shadows* had a list of Eve's friends. Mom must be on that list as well.

All Philip had wanted to do was open an investigation into his mother's death. Somehow that simple request had turned into an assault on Mr. Hale, Henderson fleeing the country, and her and Gila being shot at.

And who knows what they'd been planning to do to her mother.

According to Henderson, Philip had awakened dark entities that should've been left sleeping.

But now that they were awake, what did they want? Not her, since they tried to end her life yesterday. Was it Philip? Is he the one they wanted? That's what his father had said.

Magen Security would never let that happen. And neither would Philip.

But maybe this G character knew that and decided to harm the people around Philip instead. Threatening them until Philip did their bidding.

But what did they want him to do?

Chapter 16

Eve opened her desk drawer and searched for the notebook she jotted songs down in. When she found it, she tweaked the chorus on the one she and Roger had been working on and then added a few lines. She flipped the page over. A new song bubbled in her spirit, but she quickly put the pen down. She didn't want to write. She wanted to sing.

She looked at the bank of security monitors to her left. Eitan and Samuel were doing their hourly security check of the outside perimeter, and Philip was working in the home office. Gila wasn't on any of the indoor or outdoor monitors, which most likely meant she was tending to the bandage on her arm in one of the bathrooms.

Eve walked downstairs and made her way to the great room. Between the red brick fireplace and the large picture windows that showed a cloud-filled sky, was a baby grand piano. A Steinway, given to her by Philip on their first wedding anniversary. It was decades old and had seen better days, mainly because she played it often. Philip had offered to replace it with a newer model, but she'd declined. She had a newer one in her music room, a space they'd added in the basement for her recording sessions. She slid her fingers across the keys. This one may have been old, but it was special to her. It was for personal use, not professional.

Sadness and worry had greeted her this morning. First, she'd informed a mother of her son's death, and then she'd worried whether her neighbors were working with people who wanted her dead. People who also might have plotted to bring harm to her mother.

It was time to change the narrative.

She adjusted herself on the bench and played *A Mighty Fortress is Our God,* a favorite hymn. She sang the song over and over again, the lyrics penetrating her soul as her voice rose with each chorus. She then transitioned to *How Great Thy Art,* belting out the chorus. She continued singing until the lyrics and music blended into a soft melody. When it was finished, she clasped her hands together and marveled at how easily the two hymns had shifted her perspective from victim to victor. She and Philip were not alone in this battle. They weren't even fighting it. The battle was the Lord's.

"Wow. That was … amazing."

Eve gasped and spun on the bench toward the voice. It was only her and the Lord in the room when she'd started playing, but apparently, she'd had more than an audience of One.

Gila continued. "I had no idea you could sing like that."

"Honey, I don't know how," Philip said. "But your voice gets better by the day."

Eitan stared at her before shifting his gaze to the floor. Had he also enjoyed her singing? She couldn't tell. However, there was no mistaking the huge doggy smile Samuel was giving her.

Heat filled her cheeks. "I'm sorry. I … I thought I was alone."

Philip's eyes beamed at her. "You were until those hymns, and your voice brought us here."

She chewed her lip. She knew where Philip stood with the Lord, but she had no idea where Eitan and Gila stood. She didn't even know if they were Christians.

It was apparent Gila had enjoyed the music, but Eitan looked as though he'd rather be somewhere else. She hadn't planned her private worship session to turn out this way, but what a perfect opportunity to ask the brother-sister duo about their faith.

She was about to speak when Eitan cleared his throat. "We heard about the Smiths' phone call to your Mom."

Worry once again clawed at her. She closed her eyes and hummed the notes of *A Might Fortress is Our God,* reminding herself of the lyrics that had ushered in peace minutes before.

"Honey," Philip laid a hand on her shoulder. "You okay?"

She nodded and turned to Eitan. "The last time I talked to Mom, she said she was staying with a couple of your agents at a hotel in St. Louis. She's still okay, right?"

"Your mom's fine, but we've learned additional things about the ..." He used his fingers to make air quotes. *"Smiths."*

Philip shook his head. "Why am I not surprised that isn't their real name?"

Eitan continued. "The police found a briefcase in one of the Econoline vans. There was a folder in there that contained email messages from The Smiths. They're definitely a part of *Legion* and answer to that G character."

Eve straightened. "But they were our neighbors before any of this started."

"We know, and from what the authorities have been able to piece together so far, it appears the Smiths were sent here to keep an eye on Philip before he even asked about an investigation into his mother's death."

"But why?"

Eitan looked at Philip. "Besides your wife, who else have you told that you suspected Henderson of killing your mother?"

"No one. I never would've ..." He muttered something under his breath then added, "There was that one night."

Eitan sat in the chair across from the piano bench. "What night?"

"It was a few years ago, at an office party in a bar downtown. I'd had too much to drink and started spouting off random things. When my buddy Howard was driving me home he asked if I really thought my Dad had killed my mom. That's when I realized the extent of everything I'd said at the bar. I brushed it off and told Howard that it was just my resentment toward my Dad and the liquor that made me say all those things. But the bar was crowded that night." He rubbed the back of his neck. "I was also talking really loud. There's no telling who else might've heard it."

"Do you think your friend Howard would've told—"

"No, never."

"Then someone else must've heard it," Eitan said. "And went straight to *The Shadows.*"

Philip plopped down on the bench next to Eve. "I'm so sorry, honey. I can't believe I was so stupid."

"There's nothing to apologize for. You were just letting off steam. You had no idea someone would take what you said back to a group of people your father worked for. You didn't even know that group existed."

"I brought those people to our door, Eve. They're right across the blazing street."

She lowered her head. It had been almost two years since Philip had snapped at her like that.

And how long had she been keeping track of his last outburst?

She hadn't even known she'd been doing it.

She sighed. There was a part of her, a small part that she'd pushed away time and again, that wondered what it would take for Philip to revert to his old way of handling things. Well, she'd found her answer.

"Don't you see?" He shot up from the bench. "It isn't just my Dad and grandfather who are responsible for this mess, it's me, too. I had a hand in it." He pivoted on his heel toward Eitan. "So, now what?"

Before Eitan could answer, Philip held up a hand. "Excuse me, Eitan. Give me a minute."

He sat on the bench again and placed a hand on her thigh. "The way I just responded to you was uncalled for." He shook his head. "You didn't deserve that. I'm sorry, and I promise I won't do it again."

She hoped her shocked reaction only registered with Philip, but when she glanced at Eitan and Gila, they looked surprised as well. Samuel wasn't though. His demeanor was calm, but not his eyes. He looked like he wanted to eat Philip alive.

She swallowed because she didn't know what to say. Before, when he'd snap at her, not only would he *not* apologize, but he'd make her feel guilty for making him snap at her in the first place.

This was different. Not only was he apologizing, he was doing it immediately after the fact. Now she wouldn't have to worry about walking on eggshells around him, afraid of what would set him off next.

The tension in the air evaporated.

She reached for his hand and bit back the words, "*Don't worry about it. It's okay,*" which was the way she'd responded in the past on those rare occasions he did apologize. Back then, she didn't care. All she'd wanted to do was get back in Philip's good graces and move on with their lives.

It took her years to realize that she'd been giving him permission to mistreat her.

They'd come too far. She wasn't going to risk her happiness and their reconciliation by falling back into old patterns.

"You're right, I didn't deserve that. I was only trying to help. I appreciate you acknowledging that and apologizing." She lifted his hand and kissed it. "Apology accepted."

He smiled and mouthed the words, *thank you*, then gave her a tender peck on the lips before returning his focus to Eitan.

"So, the Smiths. Have they been arrested?"

"No."

Philip straightened. "What?"

"They haven't committed a crime."

"But you said those email messages proved they moved across the street from us on purpose."

"They did, but moving across the street from someone isn't a crime."

"They were spying on us."

"More than likely, but the police haven't been able to find any evidence of that."

Eve leaned in. "What happened to the Youngs?"

"Who?"

"The elderly couple who lived there before the Smiths. They'd been in that house for decades and had mentioned plenty of times that they had no intention of moving, then suddenly they were gone."

She stopped talking and held her breath. She hoped nothing had happened to the Youngs. Not only had they been the best neighbors, but they were also really nice people. She received a postcard from them shortly after they moved, but now she feared it was the Smiths who'd sent it to keep her, Philip, and the rest of their neighbors from inquiring about their whereabouts.

Eitan went to the kitchen table and flipped open a folder. "It says here the Habakkuk Police have confirmed the whereabouts of Mr. and Mrs. Young. They moved to Topeka to be closer to their son." He lifted his brows. "It also says the Smiths brought the Youngs' home for three times more than it was worth. That would've been a good motivator for selling."

She released the breath she'd been holding. Thank God, the Youngs were okay. Their son had health problems, so no doubt they jumped at the opportunity to be closer to him, especially if they were able to help him out financially. She was relieved that the Smiths hadn't killed them and buried their bodies in the backyard.

When Eitan closed the folder, Philip repeated his earlier question. "So now what?"

"Now we wait for this G person to show his hand because no one knows where to find him. That's where we are. You're not safe until the police locate him or he tries something else."

"He *tried* to kill my wife."

"Unfortunately, none of his henchmen lived long enough to tell us anything." He looked at Eve. "Unless that Patrick fellow said something to you last night?"

She shook her head. She hadn't even thought to ask him.

"Figures. Men like that usually take what they know to the grave."

"What about the Smiths?" She asked. "Surely they would know where to find him?"

"I'm sure they do, but they're claiming their email account was hacked. Until that's proven false, their lawyer keeps telling the police that his clients have no idea who G is."

"That's just great," Philip said. "So we're back to waiting until they try something else."

"You don't have to worry about the Smiths anymore. They know that we know who they are, so they aren't going to try anything. That call to your mother was a desperate attempt, and it failed. I wouldn't be surprised if they leave the area in the next few days." He cleared his throat. "However, I do believe they were the reason you were attacked on the road. I believe they gave that G fella a heads-up that you and Gila were leaving the home. That would also explain why there haven't been any attacks on you guys here. They know you've hired us. I'm sure the minute we pulled up, G knew about it."

"They had the perfect view. All they had to do was look out the window."

He nodded. "I'm also willing to bet it was Mr. Smith who called your wife on the phone the day she found Mr. Hale in her trunk."

Eve grabbed Philip's hand. Of course. How else would the caller have known what was going on? She gasped. "Eitan, do you think he was the one who beat up Mr. Hale?"

"I don't think so." He shrugged. "Not directly anyway. According to the police, Mr. Hale said he was approached by a young man in his mid-to-late twenties. The man told him he had extra pairs of tennis shoes and athletic socks in his car and asked if he'd be interested. Mr. Hale said yes, but as they walked past an alleyway, he was pulled into it. He doesn't remember anything after that. Unfortunately, the only business that has a security camera in that area is yours, and Mr. Hale was on the opposite end of the block."

Eve clicked her tongue. That was because there was essentially zero crime in that part of town. No business wanted to pay for security cameras if they didn't need them. The only reason her mother had them installed was because of one of her customers. She'd refused one of his advances, and he'd replied with something crude, so she'd banned him from the cafe. However, he kept showing up. She eventually showed the footage to the police. After that, he stopped coming in.

That was several years ago, but since her mother had already paid for the system, Eve had decided to keep it running.

She was glad that she did. Eitan and Gila were able to tap into that system and monitor the café from their computers.

Gila joined Eitan at the kitchen table and grimaced. The doctor at the hospital had written her a prescription for painkillers. Eve had found that prescription ripped in half in the main floor's bathroom trash last night.

It was obvious she was still in pain.

After a few seconds, Gila spoke. "Even though the Smiths will no longer be a problem, we can't assume that you or your home are no longer being watched. You and Philip can continue to stay here, or we can set you up somewhere else. Let us know. It's up to you."

Philip looked at Eve. "Honey, what are your thoughts?"

"I don't see the point in leaving. They'll just follow us."

Gila and Eitan's phones and watches beeped. Gila tapped her watch. "Well, isn't this interesting? A *For Sale* sign has just been placed in The Smiths yard, and they're loading boxes into their car as I speak." She chuckled. "That was fast."

"And," Eitan added. "Well, let's just say I have an idea, but I'll have to talk to the boss first. Let me call Dad."

Eve looked at Philip. He'd been right. Joseph Pearl, head of the Magen Midwest Agency, was indeed Eitan and Gila's dad.

Eitan pulled out his phone and walked onto the back deck.

Gila studied them. "I'm guessing the two of you have figured out that Joseph Pearl is our father."

Philip nodded. "Why didn't you tell us that in the beginning?"

"Because it has caused issues with clients in the past."

"I don't understand."

"Some clients aren't comfortable with us being related. They think we'd put each other's lives above theirs."

"Would you?"

"We're very good at what we do, Mr. Stockton. We know how to protect your lives and ours at the same time."

"That didn't answer my question."

"If Eitan and I ever have to choose between saving each other or saving one of you, it's gonna be you, our clients, every time."

"You'd save my life over your brother's?"

"Yes. And it wouldn't be the first time I've had to choose the life of a client over Eitan or Dad. And the same goes for them."

Eve chewed her lip. Was that why Eitan had made sure she was okay before checking on Gila? Even though his sister was the one who'd been shot?

Gila smiled at her. "Don't worry. My family and I will always have each other's backs, but when the chips are down, we know what has to be done."

"Still," Eve shook her head. "A father choosing someone he just met over his own son or daughter—"

"My father no longer works in the field. He's in his mid-seventies now, but he's spent over half of his life protecting others. He sees it as a ministry. Eitan and I grew up surrounded by people like him and by those they've protected. We've seen too many miracles to see it as anything other than that."

"Ministry?"

Gila nodded.

"Your dad's a Christian?"

"Yes, and so am I. Eitan is too, however he's been struggling with God for a while now. Their relationship is … complicated."

"How so?"

"Thirty-two years ago, when we still lived in Israel, our mother was out shopping when a suicide bomber entered the store and blew it up. There were ten people inside that building. No survivors. Eitan was fifteen at the time, and I was twelve. He still struggles with the way our mom died. There are seasons when he seems completely at peace with it. Then there are other times, like now, where he questions why God let her die at all."

Eve could relate. She couldn't begin to count the times she'd cried out to the Lord in the early years of her marriage, asking why He hadn't softened Philip's heart toward her. Why He hadn't intervened mightily in her marriage. And why, with each passing year, He'd let Philip's tirades and tantrums spiral more and more out of control.

But there was one question she'd asked, that she didn't care to hear the answer to. But to this day, decades later, still reared its ugly head without warning.

Why had God allowed her to lose control of her car in that horrid storm all those years ago?

And why hadn't He protected their unborn child?

She shivered as she remembered the look on the doctor's face and his solemn tone when he'd told her that their unborn son, whom she'd secretly named Abraham, hadn't survived the crash.

She blinked away tears. The Lord's response to her back then was, *I'm here. Trust Me. Hold on.*

And she had.

Until her obstetrician told her she'd never be able to carry a child to term. That the impact on her body from the accident had been too severe.

That's when her grip slipped, and she fell into a dark, despairing pit she didn't think she'd ever climb out of.

God stretched out His hand again, and she rejected it.

When voices in the darkness had started talking to her, saying she was useless as a wife and that she alone was responsible for Abraham's death because she was too stupid to realize how dangerous the roads were, and that she should end her life to rid the world of her miserable existence—she'd picked up a razor blade and slit her wrist.

When her vision had blurred and her heart rate had slowed, the Lord stretched out His hand again. She'd grabbed it and held on tight.

Then she'd fallen asleep.

When she awoke, she was at her friend Lydia's house, lying on Lydia's bed, being tended to by Lydia.

Before she'd even picked up the razor, the Lord had prompted Lydia to go see her friend. When she saw what Eve had done, she put Eve in the backseat of her car and drove to her home, where Eve stayed for an entire month.

Lydia had called Philip and told him that Eve would be staying with her for a while. He said he didn't care if she ever came back. She never told him that Eve had tried to take her life. To this day, he still didn't know.

But God had kept His promise. He'd told her to *hold on* and trust Him. She couldn't imagine that the Philip sitting next to her now would ever say anything so cold.

And she had a hard time reconciling the fact that he was the same Philip who'd refused to come to the hospital after she'd lost their son.

They served a miracle-working God. If He was able to soften Philip's heart of stone, He certainly could heal Eitan's broken one.

"You okay, honey?"

She looked at Philip. "I was just thinking about Eitan. I'm fine."

"You sure? You kind of left us there for a minute."

"Sorry. I was just—"

"We now own the house across the street." Eitan closed the door to the deck behind him. "And by *we,* I mean the

Magen Agency."

Philip's head jerked back. "What?"

"We purchase homes in various locations to use as safe houses for clients. We already have one on the south side of Habakkuk, near where your friends Ethan and Mary live. My dad thought it would make sense to have one on the north side as well. The Smiths just sold their home in a cash deal with one of our real estate investors. The lawyers are still handling the legal stuff, but as of right now the house is ours."

Eve couldn't believe what she was hearing. Now she wouldn't have to wonder if someone who wanted to harm her or Philip would be able to sneak into the place.

Eitan sat on the couch across from them. "The Smiths are only taking a handful of things. The furniture wasn't theirs anyway. The Youngs had left it for them to use. They've promised to be out of there by the end of the day. After that, our tech team will sweep it for any devices such as hidden cameras or microphones. Once that's done, we can move your mom in temporarily with one of our agents."

Eve gasped. "Oh, my word. I'd love that." She turned to Philip. "I'd feel so much better knowing Mom is close. We'll be able to afford that, right?"

He smiled. "Of course."

Eitan stood and pulled out his phone again. "I'll make the arrangements."

Chapter 17

A piano ringtone echoed down the stairway.

Eve stood. Philip, Eitan, and Gila continued their conversation about the house across the street.

"Excuse me, everyone. That's my phone. I left it in the bedroom."

She jogged up the stairs, grabbed her phone, and glanced at the display. It was Mary. She tapped the answer button.

"Hey. We were just talking about you."

"Was it in regards to the new safe house?"

"You know about that?"

Mary chuckled. "News spreads fast around here. My dad told me about it. Your PPA's are talking with his PPA's all the time."

Ezra, Mary's adopted father, was frequently in Missouri conducting business and often made it a point to stop in Habakkuk to visit the Melsons, his daughter's biological family.

Eve wasn't sure what Ezra did for a living. Well, it wasn't even for a living since he was a retiree. Mary had told her that he was a consultant of some sort, but Eve didn't know much more than that. Whatever it was, it was dangerous enough for him to need twenty-four-hour protection.

"I can't believe you've been here over a month, Mary, and

I've only had the chance to see you once."

"I know, and that's why I'm calling. Are you up for a visit? And don't worry about my safety. Now that the Smiths are leaving, they're no longer spying on your home. And even if they were, I've become the queen of disguises."

Eve laughed. "I'd love to see you, but are you sure?"

"Yep. I'll be there in a few minutes."

Eve texted Gila that Mary would be arriving soon, then went back down to the kitchen. She filled a tea kettle and placed it on the stove, then opened a package of shortbread cookies from the pantry and spread them on a plate.

When Mary arrived, Gila ushered her into the kitchen and retreated to the living area.

Eve hugged her friend. "I've missed you."

Mary returned the hug. "I've missed you, too." She pulled out a chair. "The kids and I are returning to Delaware the day after tomorrow, but I wanted to check in with you before we left. How are things?" She tilted her head toward Philip, who'd given her a quick wave before heading to his office.

Eve appreciated Philip's gesture. He'd slowly been trying to get back into the good graces of her friends. The wave to Mary was an improvement. In the past when she'd have friends over, he'd rant and rave about her spending time with them instead of cleaning the house. Their home was always clean, and Philip knew that. He'd just been looking for ways to embarrass her.

Mary knew about the changes in Philip, but she hadn't seen him in a long time. Which was probably why she didn't return his wave. She wasn't sure how he'd react.

"We're okay, considering the circumstances. And of course, Philip's dealing with a lot. Finding out the truth about his mother's death, and now having to face the fact that his father may spend the rest of his life in prison. His great-grandfather was the one who opened the door to all this madness. And oh, did I tell you about the sister Philip never knew he had?"

Mary leaned forward. "*What?*"

The tea kettle whistled. Eve turned it off and poured steaming water over the tea bags she'd left in mugs on the counter. She handed Mary one of them, then placed the other and the cookie platter on the table before resuming her seat.

She then explained about Philip's great-grandfather, grandfather, and Kaloni.

Mary shook her head. "Wow. I knew his family had something to do with this, but I didn't know the extent. And a sister? You're right, Philip is having to deal with a lot." She narrowed her eyes. "He's not taking it out on you though is he?"

She looked her friend in the eyes. She needed Mary to know she was being truthful. "No, Mary. He's not."

Mary relaxed in her chair. "Good, because before I drove over here, I called Joseph Pearl. I wanted him to know that I was going to ask Eitan to take Philip out if I found out that he was."

"Take him out, as in ...?"

Mary hiked a brow.

Eve laughed. "You didn't!"

Mary smiled but didn't deny it.

Eve chuckled and removed the tea bag from her cup. "Sounds like you've been spending a lot of time with Christianna and Windy."

Christianna was Mary's younger sister, and Windy was Kite Eagle's twin. Both were well known in Habakkuk for not taking gruff from anybody.

Mary giggled. "The past two days, actually. How'd you guess?"

"The lingo. I can't tell you how many times I've heard them talking about *taking someone out.*"

"I know, right? They always did like to walk on the wild side."

"Well, thank God they never acted on any of those threats." Eve sipped her tea. "How is Christianna these days?"

"She's still baby sissy Chrissy, full of life and excitement, though she's mellowed some. She and Brad just celebrated their twentieth wedding anniversary."

"Oh, please tell them I said congratulations."

"I will."

"And the girls?"

"Their girls are doing great. Sara will be entering university soon, and Rose is not far behind her. Time flies by so fast."

"It does." Eve took another sip of her tea. Abraham would've been in his early thirties if he'd lived. What would his life have looked like? Would he have gone to college? Gotten married? Had children?

"You okay, Eve?"

Mary's voice brought her back to the present. "I'm sorry about that. I've been getting lost in my thoughts lately."

Mary glanced back at the stairs before turning again to Eve. "Are you *sure* everything's okay? You know you can talk to me, Eve. And you don't have to sugarcoat it."

She needed to get her act together. If she didn't, Mary was going to think she was hiding something and blame Philip for it.

"Everything's fine. Really. God's been working on Philip for quite a while, Mary. He's not the same person he was before."

She sighed. "I know. Ethan said the same thing."

Ethan was Mary's husband. When he was in town, he often asked Philip to golf with him.

Mary lowered her head. "I apologize for being skeptical."

"You've witnessed some pretty intense situations between me and Philip. I understand."

"I'll try to do better."

"Thanks. And I'll let you know if he takes a turn for the worse."

Mary laughed and then said. "You know, I wonder … do you think Philip would be up for a couple's trip?"

Eve frowned. "I don't know. I think he would if it involved you and Ethan."

"It would. After the local newspapers shared my story on how I was reunited with my biological family, I was approached by an organization that focuses on missing and exploited children. At first, I wasn't emotionally ready to volunteer with an organization like that, but a year ago, I did.

"Next summer, Ethan and I are hosting an event for the organization in Hawaii. They weren't able to find me after I was kidnapped, but they've found thousands of others. Ethan and I just wanted to do something for the people who work so hard and see so much. But we'd also like our friends to join us for some fun and sun as well. Do you think Philip would be interested? Kite, Pris, Lyd, and all of the guys will be there too."

"We've never been to Hawaii, so he might be interested." She scooted her chair back. "I'll go ask him."

Mary nodded as Gila sprinted into the kitchen and wrapped an arm around Eve's elbow. Her eyes were tight. "We have a situation."

Eitan appeared out of nowhere, jogged up the steps, and returned with Philip.

"What's going on?" Philip asked.

Eve's stomach clenched. "I don't know."

Gila pointed to the couches in the great room. "We need to talk. Now."

Chapter 18

Eve hugged Mary goodbye and sat on the couch next to Philip.

Gila huffed out a breath. "I thought the two of you said you'd told us everything."

Philip nodded. "We did. After we told you about Dinah, there was nothing else to tell."

Gila looked at Eve. "Is there anything *you* forgot to tell us?"

"What?" Eve looked at Eitan. He looked just as angry as his sister. She flicked her eyes back to Gila. "Like my husband said, we're not holding back on anything else. And *I'm* not holding back on anything either."

Gila tugged her phone from her pocket. "We've been monitoring the café."

Eve nodded. "We know."

"About twenty minutes ago, a suspicious-looking young man walked up to the door. We alerted the police. They responded immediately and asked why he was there. He said he was told to leave a note on the café's door. Sgt. Dodge sent us a photo of the note. It was addressed to you."

Someone had left her a note? On the door of the café? Was it a vendor? That wouldn't make sense. She'd contacted them the day after she closed it down. Maybe it was one of her employees, or a customer asking when they'd reopen.

From the looks on Gila's and Eitan's faces, it wasn't any of the above. She blew out a breath and rubbed her temples. "What did the note say?"

Gila tapped her phone. "It says, *Have you checked on your boyfriend lately? If not, you should. And take the coroner. Your boyfriend paid a heavy price for your husband's attempts to thwart us.*"

Eve swallowed. Who in the world would leave her a note like that? And why would they say she had a boyfriend?

Gila slid the phone back into her pocket. "You should've told us you were having an affair, Eve."

Eve shot out of her seat. "I didn't tell you because I'm not!"

"The note was addressed to you."

"I don't care."

Philip reached for her hand. She gave it to him, and he gently squeezed it. "Do you think they may have been talking about Roger?"

She gasped.

Gila folded her arms across her chest. "Who's Roger?"

Philip stood. "A college friend of ours who's also Eve's music producer. They work closely together, sometimes late into the night, but they're *not* having an affair."

"And you're sure of this because ...?" Eitan asked.

"It's a long story, but my wife has been faithful. However, if someone had been following her, it would've been easy for them to think that she and Roger were an item."

"Where does Roger live?"

Philip rattled off his address. "You may want to check his studio as well. It's the only brick building on the corner of Main and Elm. You can't miss it.

Eitan called Sgt. Dodge.

Philip wrapped an arm around Eve. The room around her swirled, and he lowered her back onto the couch. She shuddered out a breath and gripped his hand. "Coroner. They said take the coroner." Her voice pitched on the last word. *It couldn't be. Not Roger. Oh, God. Please, no.*

Philip laid her head on his chest.

Gila cleared her throat. "Eve," her tone was softer than before. "When was the last time you saw Roger?"

"At his studio, a week before this madness with Henderson started." She sniffed. "After the incident with Mr. Hale, we met virtually on Friday mornings." She pushed off of Philip's chest. "He didn't show up for the meeting this morning. I didn't think anything of it since he has to schedule studio time around his artist's schedules. I thought maybe one of them popped in this morning and wanted to record while they were in town. Now I'm wondering if he missed our meeting because …" She pressed her lips together. No. She wasn't going to say it.

"Is there any other reason he might've missed the meeting?" Gila asked. "A conference out of town maybe, or—"

Eve shook her head. "He travels a lot, but he always lets his artists know when he's not going to be available."

"Is he married?"

"Divorced."

"Maybe he's somewhere with his ex?"

Could be. Out of Roger's five ex-wives, his third wife, Mackenzie, was the one he remained the closest to. Roger wasn't a Christian, and as far as she knew, neither was Mackenzie. Several times during their virtual meetings, she'd seen Mackenzie in the background or heard her voice. It was obvious by the way they talked to each other that any animosity between them had been resolved. But that was only a guess. Roger never explained why Mackenzie was always at his house, and she never asked.

"One of his ex-wives, Mackenzie, is a lingerie model and travels internationally. They've been pretty close lately, so yeah, I could see him sprinting off with her somewhere."

Eve closed her eyes. Even though it wasn't the best-case scenario, she hoped it was true. Mackenzie was known for partying hard and indulging in everything that came with that lifestyle. Roger didn't drink or do drugs, which was one of the reasons he divorced Mackenzie in the first place. But if they were together, she didn't care what they were doing, as long as he was alive.

Eitan placed a hand over his phone's microphone. "Officers are at both locations. The studio has been demolished. Sgt. Dodge said it looked like someone took a bat to all the equipment. However, Roger wasn't there."

"Thank God." Eve breathed out.

Eitan rubbed the back of his neck. "They found Roger at his home," he paused, and Eve's heart raced. After a few seconds, he looked directly at Eve. "He was shot multiple times and rushed to the hospital, but—"

Her body trembled. "But what?"

"They've had to restart his heart multiple times. He's alive, but it doesn't look good. I'm sorry."

"No. I can't lose him." She twisted in her seat toward Philip. "If he dies, I swear I'll never forgive you. This is all your fault. Yours and your stupid father's."

Philip's gaze shifted to the floor, and his jaw tightened. There was a lot he probably wanted to say, but she didn't care to hear it. She stood. "Gila, take me to see, Roger." She wiped at the tears streaming down her face. "He's suffering and alone. He needs me."

Eitan exchanged glances with Gila and then looked at the phone in his hand. "Um …"

Eve wiped at her face again. "What?"

"According to Dodge, Roger's not alone. His wife is with him."

"What are you talking about? Roger's not married."

"Does the name Maddie or—"

"Mackenzie?"

"Yes, that's it. Mackenzie Roarke."

Roarke? When they married, Mackenzie had refused to take on Roger's last name. She'd kept the one she was known by in the fashion world, Mackenzie Swan. Had they remarried, and she'd taken on his name this time around?

Eitan continued. "She was there when it happened, said four men busted through their door while they were having breakfast. They grabbed Roger, hit him over the head with a brick, then shot him multiple times. When she screamed, they covered her mouth with a rag and dragged her into the bedroom. Dodge said there was chloroform on the cloth. Mackenzie doesn't know how long she was out, but when the officers got there, she had duct tape over her mouth, and her hands and feet were tied."

Eve couldn't believe what she was hearing. "Please tell me she's okay. That they didn't—"

"We don't know all of the details yet, but as of right now, besides the rope marks on her wrists and ankles, there are no other obvious signs of assault. A female officer tried to take her to get examined, but she refused and said she wasn't leaving her husband's side. So Mr. Roarke is not alone. She rode with him in the ambulance to the hospital, and she's there with him now."

Heat flooded Eve's cheeks.

She felt like an idiot.

And the silence that permeated the room intensified the feeling.

Why hadn't Roger told her that he and Mackenzie had remarried? Roger always talked to her about everything. Why had he kept that a secret?

She dropped onto the couch next to Philip. She leaned against him, and his body tensed. Was he mad at her?

Probably.

Could she blame him? Her behavior had been embarrassing. Not only to Philip, but also to her character, and more importantly her Christian witness.

How had she allowed herself to lose all sense of control and dignity like that?

Eitan resumed his phone conversation with Sgt. Dodge and quietly walked outside.

Gila said she'd be in her room if Eve needed her.

Eve laid her head against the back of the couch. She still

wanted to go see Roger. She wanted to hold his hand and let him know that she was there.

She wanted to comfort him.

Urge him to hold on because she couldn't lose him.

She squeezed her eyes shut, damming in another torrent of tears.

Had she no shame? Roger wasn't her husband; he was her friend.

A dear friend, but there was no denying the tugs on her heart went deeper than that.

And they were definitely not Christ-like.

Philip turned her head toward him. "Look at me, Evie."

She shook her head.

"It's okay. I understand. We can talk about it if you like, but let's do that later. Right now, we need to go see our friend."

Tears spilled onto her face. "Oh, my word. I've been so wrapped up in my feelings I haven't even thought about how you were feeling. Roger's one of your oldest and dearest friends."

He pulled a crumpled napkin from his jeans pocket and dabbed at her cheeks. "Like I said, I understand."

"I'm sorry about the way I reacted earlier. It was embarrassing."

He nodded.

"Did you know that Roger and Mackenzie had gotten back together?"

"No, I didn't."

"Are you telling me the truth?" She narrowed her eyes. "Is that why you were okay with Roger and me working together again?"

"Eve." The harshness of his tone surprised her, and she clamped her lips together. He then looked into her eyes. "Hear what I'm saying to you. I. Did. Not. Know."

She ran a hand through her hair. "I'm sorry. My feelings are all over the place right now."

"You'll feel better after we see Roger."

"Probably." She swallowed back a sob. "But I can't go. It

wouldn't be appropriate."

"What do you mean?"

"Mackenzie. I'm not sure how much she knows about what happened between me and Roger. If she knows that he was secretly in love with me for years, including the years they were married, then it would be awkward. And she's just come through a horrific experience. I don't want to upset her any more than she is already."

"I get it. But if Roger doesn't make it, you'll never forgive yourself for not being there."

"Don't say that."

"Say what?"

"That he won't make it."

"Honey, you heard what Eitan said. They had to restart—
"

She lifted a hand. "Stop it. Please."

He scooted away from her. "Fine. Is there anything you'd like for me to tell him?"

"Just that," her voice quivered. "I'm praying for him."

"You know Roger's not a Christian."

She opened her mouth, but words wouldn't come out. Roger knew all about God, Jesus, and the Bible. Over the years, they'd had numerous in-depth discussions about all three. But none of that mattered because Roger adamantly refused to acknowledge that he needed a Savior.

Philip's voice broke through her thoughts. "I'm gonna let Eitan know that I want to go see Roger. Are you going to be okay?"

"Yeah, but uh, if they let you see him, just make sure you pray with him."

"I will." He stood and kissed the top of her head. "I'll call when I find out more."

When the door clicked behind him, she grabbed the nearest throw pillow, plunged her face into it, and sobbed. She didn't want Gila to hear her bawling and come running. She didn't want to have to explain something she didn't understand herself.

Especially since Gila hadn't looked at all convinced that there hadn't been something going on between her and Roger.

"Lord, thank You that Mackenzie's safe and that Roger's still alive," she choked back another sob. "But Roger's not in good shape. He needs help. Your help." She pulled the pillow tighter against her mouth and cried into it. "Please don't let him die. He needs more time. He's not ready." She rubbed her face back and forth against the velvety pillow. "Minister to his heart, Lord, in a way that only You can." She sniffed. "And speaking of hearts, fix mine. Something's wrong. I love Roger and always thought that was because he was my friend. But my heart aches in a way that makes me think I've felt something stronger for him than a friendship." She yanked her face away from the pillow and looked heavenward. "Am I *in* love with Roger, Lord? He's been honest with the way he's felt about me, but have I? I thought I had, but now I'm not so sure." She shook her head. "If I am in love with him, Lord, I'm not okay with that. Please replace that feeling with an appropriate one. The only person I want to be in love with is my husband. Philip's going through a lot, including his family being responsible for dragging Roger into this mess. He's the one who deserves my attention and comfort right now. Help me give it to him, Lord, because I can't do it on my own. This situation with Roger is threatening to undo me. But I can't lose Roger, Lord. I just can't."

Chapter 19

"Eve, wake up. Philip's on the phone."

Eve sat up on the couch. When had she fallen asleep?

"He's tried calling you several times. When you didn't answer, he called me." Gila handed her the phone, and Eve placed it on the speaker. "Philip, how's Roger?"

"He's out of surgery and doing a lot better. It's a good thing the officers showed up when they did. The doctors told us he'd lost a lot of blood."

"Us?"

"I'm in the ICU waiting room with Mackenzie. He's doing better but he's not completely out of the woods yet. The doctors said the next couple of days will tell them more, but they're optimistic he's going to make it."

"Are you sure?"

"Yeah. He was shot several times in his legs and abdomen. The abdominal wounds are the ones they're most concerned about. He's going to be in the hospital for a while, but yes, the doctors feel strongly that he's going to pull through."

Thank You, Lord. "And Mackenzie?"

"The nurses finally got her to agree to an exam. She put up quite the fuss, so that's how I know. When she returned she said besides a few side effects from the chloroform, she was fine. But hon, emotionally I don't think she is."

"A group of men broke into her home and shot her husband. I can't even begin to imagine what she's going through."

"I know. She was crying and yelling at everyone when I got here, but after talking with the surgeon, she calmed down a bit. Right now she's talking with the police. They think they've caught the guys. They want her to go down to the station and view a lineup."

"The men who attacked them didn't hide their faces?"

"No. I think they thought they'd be long gone before Mackenzie could free herself and call the police. Thank God, Eitan and Gila were monitoring the café. Otherwise, who knows how long Roger would've been lying there?"

Eve whispered another prayer of thanks for Roger's survival. "Have you had a chance to talk to him yet?"

"No. Mackenzie will be able to see him in a couple of hours. They asked that other visitors wait until morning."

"Oh."

"But I have some more good news. You may want to sit down for this one."

"I'm sitting."

"All right. Here it is." He cleared his throat before continuing. "Mackenzie gave her life to Christ a couple of years ago, and apparently she was able to talk Roger into going to church with her on Wednesday nights. Evie, they've been attending church together for a while now. And a few months ago, he responded to an altar call. I guess he realized he needed a Savior after all."

Joy filled Eve's soul. She wanted to jump and shout and tell the world about how her agnostic friend had finally accepted Christ.

But she couldn't. She was too stunned to do so.

"Did you hear me, Evie? Roger's now our brother in Christ."

"I heard you."

"Are you okay?"

"Yeah. Um, are you on your way home?"

"In a few, I'm waiting for Mackenzie's family to arrive. They should be here any minute though. Are you sure you're—"

"Yeah, yeah, I'm sure. I'll see you in a few. You and Eitan be careful driving home, okay?"

After a short pause, he said. "We'll be careful. See you soon. Love you."

"Love you, too."

Eve tapped the phone off and handed it back to Gila.

When Gila left the room, Eve laid back down on the couch. Before she'd fallen asleep, she'd poured her heart out to God regarding Roger. Begging God to spare him because he wasn't ready to spend eternity with Christ. And the whole time he was? How could Roger not tell her something like that? She should've been one of the first people he'd called. He knew she'd been praying for decades for his soul. Why had he kept that from her?

He hadn't even told her he'd been going to church.

And Mackenzie. Eve didn't care that they'd gotten back together. All she'd ever wanted was for Roger to find peace with God and be happy in any relationship he pursued. Yes, there was still a part of her that wondered what her life would've been like if she'd said yes to Roger after her divorce had been finalized. But Philip had asked for a second chance, and she gave it to him. The man Philip was today was proof that she'd made the right choice. She didn't expect Roger to hold a torch for her forever. He was bound to find someone, and she was okay with that. What she wasn't okay with was that he reunited with Mackenzie without telling her. Forget reuniting, he'd married her. That means there was a wedding of some kind. Even if it was small and intimate, she and Philip should've been invited. Even if Mackenzie didn't want them there, Roger still should've told her what was going on. She was more than just another one of his artists. She was his friend.

At least she'd thought she was.

She thought back to their interactions in the studio before they started meeting virtually. He'd been the same person he always was. Unlike his other artists, she'd start her sessions with him in his office. He'd drink a cup of black coffee, and she'd nurse a cup of hot tea. Then they'd laugh and talk like the old friends they were before they started working.

In all of those conversations, he never said anything about getting married again.

And he hadn't worn a wedding band.

Heat surged through her body. Roger keeping her in the dark about those things had made her look like a fool. Not only to her husband and Eitan and Gila but to God as well.

She'd prayed for the soul of a man who'd already chosen Christ. A man who should've told her he'd done so.

Earlier, she'd demanded to be by Roger's side to comfort him.

Now she wanted to strangle him.

The front door buzzed, and Philip walked inside followed by Eitan and Samuel.

"Hey." Philip made his way toward her. "You're in the same spot you were when I left."

"I fell asleep."

"That's good. You needed to rest."

"What is that supposed to mean?"

"That you're emotionally exhausted, and your body needs rest." He tilted his head. "And judging from that snappy comment, you need a lot more of it."

She bit her lip to cut off an even snappier reply.

"What's going on, Eve?"

She straightened and tossed a throw pillow onto the floor. Eitan and Samuel disappeared down the hallway. Philip sat next to her.

She folded her arms across her chest. "I'm mad."

"At me?"

"No, Roger."

Philip's brow quirked. "You are? It didn't seem that way earlier."

"Don't start with me, Philip. Please."

Confusion washed over his face. "Okay, fine. What are you mad at him about?"

"He kept me out of the loop. I had no idea he'd started going to church, got saved, or remarried."

"Why is that upsetting to you?"

"Those are big life changes, Philip. I'm his friend. I should've known. *We* should've known."

"I agree, but I'm not surprised he kept us out of the loop."

"What do you mean?"

"Roger's carving out a new life for himself. He's looking to the future. You and I represent heartache from his past. Obviously, the three of us are still friends, but he's put us in a different lane. He tells us only what he wants us to know." Philip shrugged. "And I'm okay with that."

The heat that swarmed through her body earlier, returned. "That's not true."

"What's not true?"

"Roger has *not* put me in a different lane."

"Uh, well, the fact that you didn't know about those major changes in his life, proves otherwise."

She smacked him across the face.

His shocked expression filled her with shame. She'd never hit anyone before. Ever.

Philip touched the side of his face. It was bright red. She braced for a reaction, but there was no anger in his eyes.

He didn't even stand to yell at her.

Instead, soft eyes looked back at her. And a sad countenance.

She wanted to pull him close, cover his face with kisses, and apologize for what she'd just done.

But her body refused to obey her heart.

He glanced over his shoulder, then whispered. "Why did you hit me, Evie?"

She wanted to give him an answer, but she had no idea why she'd hit him.

"Honey, talk to me. What is going on with you?"

"Nothing. Everything. All of it." She sucked in a deep breath. Eitan and Gila had to watch them constantly via the monitors, but were they listening in? They probably muted the sound, but she'd matched Philip's whispered tone just in case.

He nodded. "Our life has been crazy the past few weeks. From what happened to Mr. Hale, to my dad, the Smiths, the shootout, your mom … it's like we're surrounded by chaos, and we're just waiting for the next bomb to drop." He lowered his eyes before looking at her again. "But in all of the years we've been together, even the really bad ones where I put you through all kinds of heartache and pain, you never laid a hand on me. So why now?"

She swallowed.

"It has something to do with Roger doesn't it?"

She turned her face away from him.

He gently turned it back. "Are you in love with him?"

She tried to turn away again, but he held her chin in place. His grip didn't hurt, but it was firm. "I … don't think so. I think I was just in love with …"

"With what?"

"The way he made me feel. I always felt safe and loved and protected around him." She wiped at a tear. "And important." She shrugged. "He was okay with me being me, you know? And I guess over time that started to mean more to me than it should've. And when you said the future would look different for him and me, something inside my heart broke."

"I emotionally abandoned and verbally abused you for years, Evie. Decades. It's no wonder you felt safe with him. His words and kindness filled a void. And that falls on me. I'm the one who left you vulnerable and almost pushed you into another man's arms."

He wrapped his arms around her, and she cried into his chest. "I'm so sorry, Evie. I'm so, so sorry."

"I forgive you." Her voice quivered. "Will you forgive me?"

"For what? For wanting to feel loved and respected? No, I don't forgive you because there's nothing to forgive."

Chapter 20

Eve eased the bedroom door shut behind her and nodded good morning to Gila. The temperature outside had fallen overnight and had left an early morning chill inside the house. Eve was okay with the coolness, but judging from the heavy sweatshirt Gila wore, everyone else might not be, so she adjusted the thermostat.

She padded down the stairs to the kitchen, made a cup of hot tea, then stepped outside onto their back deck.

She lifted her face to the sky and smiled as an early September breeze lifted her hair, whipped it around, then gently lowered it back against her neck.

"Enjoying the sunrise?" Philip snuggled her from behind.

She giggled. "What are you doing up? Ten minutes ago you were sound asleep."

"I reached for you, and you weren't there." He pushed her hair to the side and kissed the back of her neck. "I miss you. Come back to bed."

To her surprise, neither Gila nor Eitan frowned upon Philip spending the night in the master bedroom. The Smiths were gone, and Mackenzie had identified the four men in the lineup who'd broken into her and Roger's home.

After that, the police used traffic cam footage to find out

where the men had come from before they went to Roger's. They'd been at an abandoned warehouse on the outskirts of town.

The police currently had the warehouse under surveillance. One of the men who'd attacked Roger said that G and a few other members of *Legion* were expected to show up there soon.

After Sgt. Dodge shared that news with them, she and Philip retired to their bedroom early.

They'd had a long relaxing evening and a very good night.

His kisses tingled her spine. Apparently, he'd planned to extend that good night into the morning.

She longed to indulge him, but that would only lead to a longer afternoon.

"How about we pick this up later?" She suggested. "You and I both know if we go back into our room, it'll be a long time before we come back out."

He chuckled. "Yeah, one of my employees asked if they should be looking for another job. They can't do their work if I don't do mine." He gave her a tight squeeze. "I guess I should get some of that work done today. Just a couple of hours. Around eleven, I'm going to go see Roger. I would love it if you came with me."

"Do you think he'll be able to sit up and talk?"

"No. Mackenzie texted this morning. She said he's yet to fully open his eyes."

Eve was glad she'd opened up to Philip about the struggles she was having regarding her feelings about Roger. She was more like herself again and not so wound up. She'd relaxed even more after her night with Philip, but she still wasn't ready to see Roger just yet.

She turned to him. "I think I'm going to wait a couple of days before I see him. When he's recovered a bit more, and we're able to communicate."

"Are you sure? He's not exactly out of the woods yet. It may be a while."

"I'm sure."

He tilted her chin up, lowered his lips to hers, and kissed her deeply. He then chuckled. "Why are you trying to stop me from going to work, woman?"

She giggled. "I haven't done anything."

"Oh, yes you have." He gave her a peck on the lips. "You just don't know it."

He quickly walked back inside.

What a crazy, dysfunctional pair they were.

She sipped her tea. After they'd agreed to forgive each other, the subject of Roger hadn't come back up again. And if Philip hadn't planned on going to see him, she doubted she would've even mentioned his name today. She needed a mental and emotional break from her feelings.

She pulled her phone from her skirt pocket and dialed Lydia. It rang once, and then she abruptly ended the call. She kept forgetting Lydia was married now, and it was way too early to call her friend.

The phone rang in her hand.

She answered, "I am so sorry, Lyd. I'd forgotten how early it was. Please tell Steady I'm sorry."

"Not a problem. We were both up anyway. How is it going? Everything, okay?"

Goodness. She'd forgotten to tell Lydia and the girls about Roger. How in the world had she dropped the ball on that one? He was a good friend of theirs, too.

She told Lydia about the guy and the note at the café, the attack on Roger and Mackenzie, their new marriage, and Roger being a Christian.

She also shared the conversation she and Philip had regarding her mixed-up feelings.

Lydia sighed heavily into the phone. "I'm sorry you had to find out those things about Roger that way. The two of you have always been close. I can understand why your feelings were hurt."

"Thanks. I'm just glad they're both okay."

"I am, too. And sharing your feelings with Philip was important. It was a brave thing to do. I know what happened to Roger had you feeling out of sorts, but sharing those feelings with your husband will turn out to be a blessing."

Eve smiled. She needed to hear that. "Thank you."

"I texted the girls about Roger and Mackenzie. They just replied back. Barry, Priscilla, Jack, and Kite are on their way to St. Matthew's now. He's able to accept visitors, right?"

"Philip's headed up there later, so I guess so. However, he's not able to communicate yet."

"I'll let them know. Steady and I are going to head up there as well. I also texted Ruth Greene. She just replied and said the prayer team is praying for him now."

Ruth Greene was the wife of Lloyd Greene, the pastor of their church. Ruth was also the head of their church's prayer ministry.

Eve shook her head. "Everything you're doing now, I should've done yesterday. But my mind and emotions were so—"

"Eve, you're talking to me, Lyd. Your best friend. I know you better than you know yourself. No explanations needed."

"Right." Eve then asked, "You're not surprised at all at the way I reacted are you?"

"Nope."

Eve chuckled. "Thanks again. Tell everyone I said hi, and that I'm looking forward to getting together with everyone once all of this is over."

"Will do. Love you. Call me later."

"Love you, too. Bye, Lyd."

Eve clicked off the phone, and Gila walked onto the deck. Gila pointed to her phone. "Eitan and I just talked with Sgt. Dodge. The police have now surrounded the warehouse."

"Did G show up there?"

"One of the cameras picked up a couple of SUV's pulling into the warehouse around midnight. They think he might be in one of them."

"Does Philip know?"

"Eitan has briefed him."

"So all of this madness could be over this morning?"

Gila's expression wasn't as hopeful as she would've liked.

"The Habakkuk Police haven't made us aware of their plans, but there's a possibility this could be over today, yes."

A possibility was good. She'd pray and hope for that.

"I know Philip was planning on going to see his friend, but until the situation at the warehouse is over, it's best the two of you remain here for now."

"That's fine. A group of friends are on their way to see Roger now. They'll let us know how he's doing."

The door to the deck yanked open. "There's a shootout at the warehouse," Eitan said. "Several officers have been hit. No fatalities, but the Habakkuk Police are outnumbered. About a hundred people are in that warehouse, and they all have weapons."

"Sgt. Dodge told you all of this?" Gila asked.

"No, I'm listening to the scanner. Reinforcements from neighboring police departments are on their way to the scene now."

Gila nodded. "I'll get our vests."

She returned quickly with three bulletproof vests. She handed one to Eitan, slid one on herself, and walked toward Eve with the other one.

"Wait. What's going on?"

Gila lifted Eve's arm and helped her into the vest. "This is just in case."

"In case of what?"

Eitan tightened his jacket. "In case the warehouse is a distraction."

"A distraction?"

He tapped Gila on the shoulder. "I'll turn on the outdoor laser alarms, then suit up Samuel and Philip."

He sprinted back into the house.

Eve adjusted the vest. "Gila, what's going on?"

"A lot of police are headed to that warehouse. Along with other first responders. Sometimes bad characters use that tactic to get emergency personnel away from the real target."

Eve's stomach churned. "Do you mean us?"

"We don't know that's going to happen, but we're taking precautions."

"Should I go back inside?"

"That's probably a good idea, but either way, you'll need to wear the vest."

Eve's phone rang. It was Priscilla.

She pressed the talk button. "Pris, I can't talk right now—"

"Eve, listen. Mama had a vision."

Eve was aware of Mabel's visions. She didn't have them often, but when she did, they were worth listening to.

Priscilla continued. "Mama saw a dark entity trying to enter your home. Not physically. *Spiritually.* Strong demonic forces are trying to permeate the premises. Her guess is that right now, there's someone, somewhere, conjuring up these forces."

Eve swallowed. "What else did she see?"

"That's it. But remember, your home is covered by the blood of Jesus, and so are you and Philip, so there's not a chance in hell that those forces will be able to break through. But we don't know if they might try to send them somewhere else or *into* someone, so stay alert and be watchful." Priscilla paused a few seconds, then continued, "Sorry, I was just talking with Lyd. Instead of visiting Roger, everyone has decided to meet here at our place. We're going to go later this evening instead. Until then, we're all going to be praying."

"Add the Habakkuk Police Department to your list. They're under attack." She explained what was happening at the warehouse.

"Covered," Priscilla said. "Because everyone here has already started praying for the whole town of Habakkuk."

Chapter 21

A loud blast echoed in Eve's ears.

Gila pushed her to the deck floor and pulled her weapon. Tornado sirens wailed.

Eve's heart raced. *What in the world was going on?*

Gila holstered her weapon. "That didn't come from a gun. Something exploded."

Several more blasts reverberated through the air.

The door yanked open again. This time it was Philip. Eitan was right behind him.

Philip dropped to his knees next to Eve. "Are you okay?" His whole body shook. "When I heard that blast, I thought … I thought—"

The warmth of his arms stopped hers from trembling. "I know. Thank God I'm fine. Gila said that wasn't a gunshot."

"It wasn't," Eitan said. "But we need both of you to get back inside. Now."

They scrambled up, and Eve looked around the deck. "My teacup?"

Gila looked over the deck railing. "It's shattered on the concrete below. It must've slid off the deck when we ducked for cover."

Her favorite teacup. Handed down to her from her great-grandmother. She sighed. She loved that cup. Thankfully, she had several more that had been handed down to her. They didn't hold the same memories that one had, but losing it was a small price to pay for not being shot at.

Her arms had stopped trembling, but her legs had not, and she stumbled into the kitchen. Philip pulled out a chair from the kitchen table for her, but she was too jittery to sit and too afraid.

Demons were trying to infiltrate her home.

She steadied herself against the counter. Did the explosions have something to do with that?

Were they even related to Mabel's vision?

And why were the tornado sirens still blaring?

She needed to stay calm. She reached for the empty tea kettle, frowned, and retrieved the phone from her pocket, instead. She pulled up the weather app. She scrolled back and forth and opened another app. No news alerts about inclement weather on either app. Besides being a bit cloudy, it was supposed to be a clear September day in Habakkuk.

She placed her phone on the counter and filled the kettle. Oh, how she wished Lydia was here. Eve wasn't as familiar with spiritual warfare as much as Lydia. Or even Mabel, for that matter. She smiled as she imagined what it would look like if Lydia and Mabel were in her home right now. They would both be walking throughout her home and praying up a storm. In English and in their heavenly languages. They would be rebuking the enemy and binding this and loosening that. Then they'd break out holy oil and anoint everyone in the house, including the dog.

She remembered when the three of them had gone grocery shopping together. On their way back to the car with their groceries, a woman appeared out of nowhere and tried to grab Mabel's purse. The three of them were able to prevent that from happening, but it didn't stop there. Lydia asked the woman if she'd like prayer. The woman was hesitant at first but eventually agreed.

The three of them laid hands on her and prayed right there

in the grocery store's parking lot. Eve generally prayed quietly when praying for someone in public, and she'd done so that day. But Lydia and Mabel had prayed loud enough for passersby to hear. A few of them even stopped to watch what was happening.

After several minutes of prayer, the woman started crying, then she wailed before slumping to the ground. Eve had taken a step back, but Lydia and Mabel knelt next to her and continued to pray fervently for the woman. Eve then heard a loud snap, like a chain being broken. Then she heard another, followed by several more. The woman then laid her head in Lydia's lap, and she and Mabel continued praying for her. It wasn't until security hurried out to see if the woman was okay, that the three of them learned the woman's name was Jessica.

Eve then told Jessica about Jesus. That was her gifting. Not spiritual warfare. But right now, she was glad she had spiritual warriors like Lydia and Mabel praying for her. Because she was too scared to pray for herself.

"Evie, please come sit." Philip patted the chair he'd pulled out. "I'll make the tea for you."

She walked to the table and looked around. Gila was in the great room on her laptop, and Eitan and Samuel were in the foyer preparing to go outside.

A loud noise filled the room. Experience told her the cause of it. It was the sound of cars colliding.

Eitan pulled his gun from the holster. "Wait here."

"I'll be watching," Gila said as she clicked away on the keyboard before making her way to the foyer. She locked the door behind her brother then turned to Eve and Philip. "I'm going to go track him and Samuel on the monitors."

All three of their phones chirped. It was Eitan. He'd texted that four cars had collided a few houses down from theirs. She squeezed Philip's hand. Ambulance sirens now mixed in with the tornado ones.

Their phones chirped again. Eitan had sent a photo of the crash. Eve gasped.

"Gila, you guys have to go help them!"

"We can't."

"What do you mean you can't? Two of those drivers looked unconscious. Eitan's a medic and—"

"Eitan took that photo from your driveway. We cannot leave the premises. Our job is to protect the two of you. Nothing can distract us from that."

"Fine, then I'll go." Eve moved toward the door. Philip grabbed her arm, and Gila jumped in front of her.

"Gila, those people need help."

Philip loosened the grip on her arm. "They need the type of help we can't give." He eased her away from the door. "But our Father can." They sat at the kitchen table, and he reached for her hand again. "Let's pray."

Philip prayed for their neighbors with an intensity she'd never heard from him before. When he paused for a breath, she tried to continue the prayer but realized she had nothing to add. He'd covered everything.

The ambulance sirens got louder, and so did the tornado ones. Eve covered her ears. Why hadn't the city officials turned off the tornado siren yet?

A red blur sped past one of their windows. That had to be a fire truck. It was followed by an ambulance going just as fast. *Thank You, Father God.*

Gila walked to the table and spoke directly in Eve's ear. "Help has arrived."

"I know."

Gila continued. "We're not heartless. Eitan and I have to consider that someone intentionally caused those accidents to pull us away from you and Philip. Please understand how we cannot let that happen."

"Will you be able to get updates on their conditions?"
Gila nodded.

"When you do, please let us know how."

"I will." She tapped the earpiece in her right ear. "I'm also listening to what's going on at the warehouse and other places around town. Those explosions came from a battery factory on Varner Road."

Varner Road was only a few miles from them. "Was anybody hurt?"

"That information hasn't been released yet."

Eve folded her hands on the table and laid her head on top of them.

Gila told Philip she was going to check on Eitan and Samuel.

When she left, Philp said, "A lot of things going on at once. Weird. Maybe Gila's right. Maybe someone is trying to pull them away from us."

"They're trying to get in."

"I know, that's what I'm saying."

Her head throbbed. "They're not trying to come through the door. They're trying to manifest themselves in our home."

"What?"

She lifted her head and told Philip what Priscilla had shared with her.

He leaned closer to her. "Do you believe that's possible? For someone to be able to conjure up spirits like that?"

"Yes. Do I think they'll be successful? No. Darkness can't overcome Light." She shuddered. "But Priscilla also mentioned that whoever is behind this may send them somewhere else if they failed to get through. That is what scares me."

"Huh." He then asked, "Do you think that's the cause of all the craziness going on around here?"

Eve shrugged. "I do, but there's no way for me to know for sure."

He pulled out his phone. "I'm calling our pastor. He'll advise us on what to do next."

"He and his wife are at Barry and Priscilla's praying with the others. Let's not bother them though until we know more."

The tornado sirens ceased.

"Thank God." Eve sucked in a breath and exhaled. "They were getting louder and louder. My head is throbbing."

"I need to see what's going on." He strode into the great room and grabbed the remote. When the television clicked on, breaking news alerts flashed across the bottom of the screen. He clicked through the local news channels.

Channel 6 talked about the tornado sirens. One reporter said a reliable source told her that a glitch in the tornado warning system was to blame for the sirens going off.

Channel 5 said that there had been an unprecedented number of car crashes and collisions around Habakkuk and that first responders were stretched to the limit.

Channel 3 had reporters on scene at the warehouse to cover the shootout. The place looked like a war zone. Numerous men and women, fully covered in body armor, shot automatic weapons at the police from different openings inside the dilapidated structure. Several neighboring police departments had answered the call for help.

Eve watched in anticipation as they surrounded the building.

But they were still outnumbered.

And outgunned.

Philip continued flicking through the stations. One showed a SWAT team deploying. Another channel talked with the leader of a group of former military guys who were livid that their beloved Habakkuk police force was under siege. Their heavily tattooed leader swore they'd even the odds.

The camera then panned and showed over a dozen men in camouflage, wearing vests loaded with weapons and grenades. The cameraman followed as they hopped inside pickups and on motorcycles. They took off one after another, dust from the road covering the camera lens.

The scene switched to the station's news desk, where the anchorwoman said the Missouri Governor was about to hold a press conference. There was talk of sending in the National Guard.

Lord, what is going on?

A dark spirit has been unleashed over Habakkuk. His name is Chaos.

Eve straightened and stared at the television. She had more questions for the Lord, but did she really want more answers?

No. She didn't.

The screen continued to fill with news of rioting, fires, and bedlam. When the station zoomed in on two men fighting in the street, Philip clicked off the TV.

He went to their couch, knelt in front of it, and bowed his head.

She did the same.

They prayed for their friends, her mom, his dad, and his sister, as well as everyone involved in the shootout at the warehouse.

Then she cried.

And cried some more.

Guilt overwhelmed her.

She and Philip were responsible for what was happening to their town.

No. She shook her head at the lie. They hadn't caused any of this.

The blame belonged to Satan, not her. Not Philip.

She wiped away the tears and prayed harder than ever for their beloved hometown.

Habakkuk needed God.

And they needed Him now.

Chapter 22

Eve opened her medicine cabinet and retrieved a bottle of aspirin.

She shook four of them into her hand, filled a glass with water, and popped them into her mouth.

They were regular strength, not extra, but she hoped the double dosage would give her the same type of relief.

Earlier, after she and Philip had prayed, they'd watched several more hours of news coverage. As she leaned her head on his shoulder, the pain in her head decreased.

Thank you, Lord.

She closed the medicine cabinet. God knew what she hadn't wanted to express out loud.

That her throbbing headache had been caused by something sinister and not an annoying tornado siren.

The fact that the pain decreased on its own as she'd sat quietly on the couch was a huge relief.

She didn't know if she would've had the strength or the knowledge to fight against whatever force might've been trying to get into her head.

Fortunately, it was just another headache.

The pain and throbbing would've increased in intensity if it had been the other. And the aspirin she'd just taken would've been useless against the attack.

Thankfully, they were already working.

How could she have let herself doubt? "O me of little faith." She rolled her eyes at her reflection in the mirror and grabbed a washcloth. After washing her face, she rubbed in a few drops of moisturizer.

Philip had decided to continue to watch coverage of the carnage, but she'd had enough. It was only eight o'clock in the evening, but she was done. The emotion of the day had taken its toll.

She'd tried for hours to get in touch with her mom and Lydia, but the calls wouldn't go through. Two of the three cellular networks in the area had simply stopped working. The other was unreliable even on the best of days, and today was no exception.

Fortunately for her and Philip, Eitan and Gila switched their phones to a private network the day they arrived, so they had service and internet when many others did not.

When she was finally able to get through to her mom, Kay had been frantic. Eitan had already told Kay's security team that her daughter was fine, but her mother wasn't satisfied until they connected her to their private system, and she was able to video chat securely with her daughter.

Eve hated seeing her mother upset like that. It tore at her heart.

Magen's tech team was scheduled to complete their sweep of the former Smith home by the weekend, two days away. Eve wanted her mom close, and having her across the street, where they could physically check on each other, would do both of their hearts good.

Eve had tried calling Lydia and the other girls several times. The only one she was finally able to get through to was Mary.

Mary had told her that others from their church had joined them at the King Estate and had decided to pray through the night. When word got out about that, several other prayer groups from various churches throughout Habakkuk did the same.

Eve slipped a nightgown over her head and debated opening the bathroom door. Once she did, she'd no longer have any privacy. When she and Philip were alone in the bedroom, the lights on the cameras switched from green to red, and the monitoring screens showing their bedroom went blank.

But ever since the first explosion, Eitan and Gila had been watching them like hawks. They apologized for not being able to extend them any further marital privacy but stressed that they needed to know where both of them were at all times. The town remained in an upheaval, and an attempted breach of the home's perimeter was still likely.

The only reason Gila wasn't outside her bathroom door right now was because every fifteen minutes, she or Eitan took turns walking through the woods behind their home with Samuel. They looked for anything out of place, or that might not have gotten picked up by the outdoor cameras.

Eve opened the bathroom door. If Gila was in the woods with Samuel, then Eitan was monitoring the indoor system. If she stayed in the bathroom too long, he'd knock on the door to check on her.

She didn't want that.

She grabbed Philip's dark blue bathrobe off the hook next to the door and entered the bedroom. After fluffing the pillows, she pulled the sheets back and slid under them.

"Hey," Philip poked his head into the room. "How are you feeling?"

She nodded against the plush pillow. "A lot better."

"Good." He smiled and entered the room. "Something just happened that you need to know about."

He was smiling, so it couldn't be bad news. Or was he just trying to get her to relax before he dropped a bombshell?

"What is it?"

"The showdown at the warehouse is over. Twenty people have been arrested, and G was one of them."

She sat up straight. "What?"

"I watched as it played out. All the local news channels covered it."

"What happened?"

"The SWAT team sent in drones and robots with smoke bombs, then rushed inside. It wasn't pretty, but it worked."

"Were any more of our officers hurt?"

"No." Philip's smile disappeared. "But a lot of the bad guys were. It's been reported that there are over a hundred dead bodies in that warehouse."

"Oh, no."

Philip shrugged. "It's sad it had to end that way, but the situation was getting out of hand. They had to do something."

"What do you mean?"

"The people inside the warehouse had an endless supply of weapons. The police had the building surrounded, but they refused to surrender. They just kept on shooting. Then, there were the militia groups that kept popping up to help the police. They needed the help, but the group leaders refused to tell their teams to follow orders. One of the groups tossed in an explosive of some kind, then charged into the warehouse commando style, guns blazing, shooting at anything that moved."

"Oh. My. Word."

"It was brutal."

She was glad she'd gone to bed early. And she made a mental note to avoid watching the news over the next couple of days. The last thing she wanted were images of the carnage dancing around in her head.

Philip continued. "Once SWAT took over, things calmed down. Everyone fell in line with their game plan."

"Thank God."

"Yeah."

"And G was arrested? He wasn't killed?"

"He's alive and in jail." Philip sat next to her on the bed and smiled. "It's over, babe. It's finally over."

She pulled him into a hug. "What do you think is going to happen next?"

"I don't know." He rubbed the back of his neck. "A lot of people died today in that warehouse. I'm sure there are going to be questions, inquiries, investigations, etc. But as far as Garringer goes, I can't see him ever seeing the light of day again."

"And the rest of Habakkuk? Is it getting back to normal?"

"Too early to tell, but there haven't been any more explosions, fires, or unexplained car crashes if that's what you mean. And that brings me to another bit of interesting news."

"What?"

"Eitan told me that law enforcement found Garringer on the top floor of the warehouse, sitting in the center of a large hexagram painted on the floor. Pastor Greene said that particular symbol is used a lot in occultic practices. And one of the main reasons they use it is to conjure up spirits."

"No way."

He nodded. "Looks like what Mabel saw in her vision was right. God is so good. Not only did He give us a heads up, He protected us."

"As always."

Philip grinned. "As always."

Eve blinked away a dark thought. The one that always reared its ugly head when she'd least expected it to. Try as she might, she couldn't get rid of it. Images of her car careening off of a slick road flashed before her eyes. God had definitely protected her that night. But why not him? Why not their unborn child?

"Evie?"

She tried to respond, but liquid salt spilled onto her lips. Tears.

No surprise there.

Whenever she thought about the child her arms longed to hold, they appeared and flowed at will.

Philip frowned. "Honey, what's wrong?"

She pulled a tissue from the decorative box next to the bed. "His name was Abraham."

His brow furrowed. "Who's name was Abraham?"

"Our son. His name was Abraham."

His eyes widened, and his mouth opened.

She stiffened and closed her eyes. Did she want to hear his response to what she'd just said? She had no idea, but she steeled her heart just in case.

Silence.

She opened her eyes just enough to see if he was still in the room.

He was.

His cheeks reddened. "I ... I didn't know you'd named him."

She nodded and dabbed at the tears. "I know."

"Abraham." He cleared his throat. "That's ... a nice name."

She nodded again.

He shook his head. "I can't believe I left you alone to deal with that. I was such a coward. I have a stronger word for my behavior back then, but I know you frown upon cursing."

"I do, but over the years, I've come up with a few colorful words of my own for how you behaved."

"You can call me them now if you'd like."

She thought about it, then clicked her tongue. "No. They're clean, but they're mean. And I don't want to argue right now."

He raked his fingers through his hair. "Would saying I'm sorry even be enough?" His tone was low and soft. "There's nothing I can do to make up for the way I treated you I know that." He sniffed. "But, oh, God, how I wish there was."

She wiped her nose with the tissue.

"I also know you weren't okay after losing him. For months, I watched you withdraw further inside yourself. You pulled away from your mother, your friends, me. You were hurting, but I didn't know what to do about it, so I lashed out at you. Anger. My go-to emotion for everything."

She nodded. "I didn't mean to bring any of that up today. It's just that I've been thinking a lot about Abraham lately. It started after we found out someone was out to get us. And every time the Lord protected us, there was always a part of my heart that asked, '*Why me? Why Philip? Why not Abraham?*'"

"Did the Lord ever answer that question?"

"He did. He said, *I'm here. Trust Me. Hold on.* And recently He's also reminded me of Psalms 34:18."

"I know that one." Philip lowered his gaze. "The Lord is near to those who have a broken heart."

"Yes. That's just one of the many ways He keeps reminding me I'm not alone, that He's with me and that no matter what happens in this life I need to trust Him. And to hold on to His hand when it all becomes too much."

"Like today."

She smiled. "Like today."

He squeezed her hand. "I want to say something, but I'm not quite sure how to say it. I don't want it to come across as insensitive."

"It's okay. Go ahead."

"I know you still long for a child, and even though I've never talked about it, I do too." He lowered his head. "I know we can't bring Abraham back but …"

"Go on."

"When I look at Barry and see the love between him and little Heidi …"

Eve chuckled. "She adores her dad."

"Do you think we could do something like that?"

"You mean adopt?"

"Yeah."

"Philip, no adoption agency in their right mind is going to let us have a child. Your dad is a criminal. Your past behavior around town is well known. Not to mention somebody tried to kill us. It's only a matter of time before all that comes out."

"We could explain all of it."

"Possibly, but then there's our age."

"Barry and Priscilla were able to adopt."

"Not really, Heidi's mom kind of hand-picked them." She waved her hand. "And they didn't go through an agency. All of that was handled by lawyers."

"Okay, we'll do the same. Surely, there are a lot of other young women going through an unplanned pregnancy. All we have to do is go pick one out."

She giggled. "It doesn't quite work that way, but I hear you. And if it's something you'd really like to look into, then I'm on board."

"It is."

"When this nightmare with Garringer and *Legion* is over, maybe we could start making a few phone calls."

"I'd like that." He smiled at her. "Garringer's been arrested. That's the first step in getting our lives back." The wayward dimple in his chin that made random appearances appeared. "You're going to make a great mom."

He kissed her tenderly on the lips, and she imagined what their life would look like with a newborn in the home. Decades ago, Philip would've been a terrible dad. Abraham had been spared that.

But now? He'd make an awesome one. Somewhere along the line, he'd learn to love. And that's all a child needs.

Her heart swelled with hope.

Could it be? Would she finally be able to hold a child of her own in her arms one day?

Chapter 23

Garringer was on the loose.

No one knew how, or even when, but Garringer had escaped.

Philip was livid.

Sgt. Dodge crossed his arms and widened his stance. Eve had offered him a cup of coffee and a seat at the kitchen table, but he'd refused, saying he couldn't stay long.

She was glad he'd be leaving soon. She liked Sgt. Dodge, but news about Garringer escaping was not how she'd planned to start her morning. The sooner he said what he had to say, the better.

"How could you let this happen?" Philip shouted at him. "The entire town watched as you walked him out of the warehouse and into your patrol car."

"Calm down."

Philip sat on the hearth and clasped his hands together. "I just don't understand how you guys had him in custody, and now you don't."

"Neither do we. He was put in a cell by himself. The surviving members of *Legion* didn't want to be in the same cell with him. They were afraid."

Philip frowned. "Of Garringer?"

"Yeah."

"Did they say why?"

"According to them, they had been given two options. Kill anyone who tried to enter the warehouse, or die trying."

"So, he's mad because they're alive?"

"According to them, he's more than mad. He's no longer there, and they're still afraid that he's going to kill them."

"Seriously?"

Sgt. Dodge nodded. "There's more. They also said Garringer has the ability to appear and disappear at will. But that he only disappears when he's been recalled."

"Recalled by who?"

"We have no idea, and neither do they. But they did say, and again, this is according to them, that if he's been recalled, that means he failed, and the mission is over."

"What mission?"

"To find your dad, kidnap you, and kill Eve."

Eve winced. She already knew about those things, but the way Dodge said it sent shivers up her spine.

He continued, "Now that Garringer's been recalled, the assignment against the three of you has been canceled." He adjusted his belt. "Again, that's according to *Legion*."

Philip looked at Eve, then asked, "They're criminals. How do you know they're not lying?"

"We don't. That's why I contacted an old friend of mine, a retired cop and expert in the occult. He's familiar with *The Shadows* and *Legion* and agrees with what the members of *Legion* are saying. So does your dad."

"You've talked with my dad?"

"Through the FBI, yes. However, none of that means we're going to stop looking for Garringer. Earlier, we received a traffic cam photo showing Garringer driving a silver Toyota Camry."

"That's great. Were the cameras able to follow him from there? Are officers on their way to that location?"

"The town he was in is located in Oregon. The state police there have been notified. They're on the lookout for him."

Philip shook his head.

Dodge continued, "I'm not buying the disappearing at will thing. I think he had help, possibly from the inside. Surveillance footage at the station doesn't confirm that, but I have my best investigators looking into everyone who was on duty last night. It may take a while, but as soon as I find out anything, I'll let you know."

Philip stood. "So, where does that leave me and my wife?"

"Personally, I don't think we've seen the last of Garringer. However, my occultic source assures me that you guys are safe." He shrugged. "Garringer may have moved on to other things, but how you decide to live your lives from now on is completely up to you." His arms fell to his sides. "Let me know if I can help with anything."

Philip mumbled something then walked him to the door. After Sgt. Dodge left, Philip locked the door and then leaned against it. "This is crazy. All of it."

"I know." Eve sat on the couch. "But what do we do now?"

He walked into the great room and sat next to her. "I say we do what we talked about last night. We take our lives back and do what God has been telling us to do all along. Trust Him and move forward with our lives."

"I like that. Walking in faith instead of fear."

"Exactly."

She smiled. "All right. What is the first thing you'd like to do?"

"First, I'd like to visit Roger. I've texted Mackenzie, but she hasn't texted back. I'd really like to see how he's doing."

"I'll go with you."

"I'd like that."

"The second thing?"

"Get the keys to my dad's Corvette and go for a long drive."

"Where would you go?"

"You mean where would *we* go? Don't know. Don't care. As long as you're by my side." He grinned. "I can see it now.

The cool temps blushing your cheeks, the wind blowing through your hair—"

"You getting pulled over for going fifty miles over the speed limit."

He chuckled. "All part of the adventure."

Eitan walked into the room, followed by Gila.

Gila spoke first. "It's nice seeing the two of you relax again."

Eitan nodded. "We were watching the monitors. We also heard everything Dodge had to say."

Philip straightened. "What are your thoughts about what we should do next?"

"I think what you said earlier is perfect. Trust God and move on with your lives." He lowered his head for a moment, then said, "Gila told me she told the two of you about our mom."

"I'm sorry you had to go through something like that," Eve said. "How are you doing?"

"God and I are on good terms today, so that's a step forward."

She smiled. "Glad to hear it."

He scratched his cheek. "It's hard moving on in life when someone who is supposed to be here isn't. Especially when they were taken away from you violently. But our mom would be disappointed if she knew it's taken me thirty years to move on."

"It's hard."

He looked her in the eyes. "It is." He then cleared his throat. "But I agree with Dodge that the next steps the two of you make should be up to you. Gila and I can stay on for as long as you like, but I don't think you need us anymore. If this Garringer character has been spotted in his home state, I suspect he's preparing to go on the run. His face was plastered all over the news this morning, so I don't think he'll be coming back here anytime soon.

"And as far as *Legion* goes, most of them are in the morgue. The remaining few that aren't are too afraid of their own shadows to do anything. And with their leader gone, I doubt they'll cause any problems."

Philip nodded. "What about you two? Do you have other clients in the area or—"

"Only if we're done here." He chuckled. "Actually, we would be working for your friend Mary's dad, Ezra Isaac. The threats against him have increased. He's given quite a few fiery speeches condemning those who have boycotted Israeli businesses. He travels quite a bit, and his PPAs could use the extra help."

Eitan had referred to Ezra as Mary's dad. Which was legally true, since he adopted her when she was younger, but John Melson was Mary's biological father. However, Eve didn't know how much Eitan and Gila knew about that situation, so she didn't correct him. But he was right about Ezra. He was a true man of God who loved the Lord, and who, at least in Eve's opinion, had missed his calling to be a traveling evangelist. When he spoke, people listened. And no matter what topic he spoke on, he always found a way to lead the listener to the Scriptures.

"Can we keep the equipment?" Philip asked Eitan, interrupting her thoughts.

"Sure. Which ones?"

"All of it. The monitors, cameras, mics, drones, alarms, private wi-fi network, the laser system. Samuel."

Eitan laughed. "Actually, you already own all of the electronic stuff. You'll see the prices for them on the invoice my dad'll send over when we're done. However, Samuel stays with us."

Philip groaned. "I figured."

The four of them laughed.

Then there was an awkward pause.

Gila broke through the silence. "So, the choice is yours. What would the two of you like to do?"

Philip extended his hand to Gila. "Thank you for saving my wife's life."

Gila shook his hand. "I'd do it again in a heartbeat. We

need more people like her in the world."

Eve blushed. She didn't know Gila felt that way about her. As a matter of fact, she'd been sure that whatever respect she may have gained from Gila early on had been trashed when the possibility of an affair with Roger had come up.

Eve gave her a hug, then the brother and sister team packed their suitcases, which were small in size compared to their weapon cases.

As they were loading their SUVs, Eitan pointed to the house across from them. "And don't forget the Magen Security Agency now owns that home. In a few days, it'll be staffed with some of our personnel since your mom doesn't need it anymore. If you have questions about safety or any of the equipment, feel free to talk with them. They know who you are. You may even see Gila and me over there once in a while. We'd love to stop back over here and say hi if we can."

"We'd love that." Eve gushed.

After they left, Philip turned to her. "Ready to go see, Roger?"

She shivered against the late September chill. "Yes."

"I'll grab your sweater, then back the car out of the garage."

When Philip ran inside, she looked down at the brick driveway. Did she just lie to her husband? She wanted to see Roger, but she wasn't *ready* to see him. She inhaled the sweet September air and hoped it would calm the sea of emotions surging inside of her.

She couldn't put off seeing Roger any longer. She needed to see for herself that he was doing well and on the mend.

And she needed to know why he'd kept so many secrets from her.

When the garage door opened, she stepped onto the lawn. It was a lot crunchier than the last time she'd stepped on it.

Philip wrapped the sweater around her shoulders. He then stepped back inside the garage to back the car out.

The sweater warmed her, but the warmth only added to the nausea building in her stomach.

Would Roger even want to see her?

Would Mackenzie?

She nibbled her lip. The last thing she wanted to do was explain or defend her relationship with Roger to anyone.

Including his wife.

She'd leave if it came to that. Even if that meant not seeing her music producer and friend.

And if that meant leaving Philip behind to explain her sudden exit, so be it.

Chapter 24

Eve had been to St. Matthew's Hospital multiple times, but she'd never seen it as busy as it was today.

There were no available spaces in the oversized outdoor parking lot or the inside one. The frazzled parking attendant told them the lot was full. The attendant then had to calm down an irate driver who had gotten out of his car and demanded to be let in.

Philip finally found a meter on Main Street. They'd parked there and walked two blocks to the hospital.

When they arrived at the main entrance, security was arguing with three young women. They had to physically move them out of the way before she and Philip could enter.

Inside wasn't much better. People were everywhere, and everyone seemed angry.

Mackenzie had texted them earlier, letting them know that Roger had been moved from the ICU, but she hadn't said where. Philip tried calling her, but the call wouldn't go through.

When they reached the information desk, Philip asked for Roger's room number. As the woman typed on her keyboard, Eve pointed to the crowd of people behind them and asked, "What's going on?"

The woman sighed loudly. "It's been this way since

yesterday morning. So many people were brought here because of car accidents, fires, and everything else that happened. Some of those people have been waiting hours to see a physician, and the Emergency Room is at capacity. We're trying to coordinate with St. Helen's, but they're having the same issues." She rubbed her temples. "It's been a nightmare."

"I'm sorry you're having to deal with all of this."

She smiled at Eve. "That's the nicest thing anyone has said to me all day." She wrote Roger's room number on a Post-It note and handed it to Eve. Before releasing the note, she said, "I appreciate you saying that. Thank you."

Eve gave her a quick smile then followed Philip through the crowd to the elevators. When the elevator arrived, there was only enough room for one person. A second one dinged, and it was empty. Philip grabbed Eve's hand and pulled her in behind him. Others followed and didn't seem to care that they were close to capacity. If there was an inch of space, someone found a way to squeeze in.

Roger was on the seventh floor. She dreaded the thought of having to squeeze by some of the people in front of them, who smelled like they hadn't showered in days. Thankfully, by the time they reached his floor, the elevator had pretty much emptied out.

When they exited the elevator, she pulled her mirrored compact from her purse. She hadn't had the chance to put on any makeup before Sgt. Dodge arrived at their home this morning, and it showed. She looked like she needed a nap. A long one.

Philip wrapped an arm around her. "You look beautiful."

She snapped the compact shut. He was trying to calm her nerves, but she had to disagree. She definitely looked like she'd seen better days. But what did it matter? She was only going to see a sick friend.

They turned down the hallway to Roger's room, and a tall woman with long, shiny dark hair stood in front of Roger's door, talking with a physician. Philip cleared his throat, and the woman turned toward them.

Mackenzie.

Not a stitch of makeup, and she looked as flawless as ever. Eve's throat tightened.

Mackenzie's eyes narrowed. "Eve."

Eve studied Mackenzie's expression. Except for her eyes, the rest of her face was expressionless. Even the way she'd said *"Eve"* didn't give her a clue of how to respond.

"Mackenzie."

She hadn't been in the same room with Mackenzie in years, but time had been kind to her. She was dressed in a pair of loose jeans and a light blue sweatshirt sporting John 3:16 across it in white.

Not the usual style of clothing she'd seen Mackenzie in before, which typically included a low-cut blouse and tight-fitting pants.

The doctor stepped away, and Philip asked, "Is everything okay with Roger?"

Mackenzie shifted her gaze to Philip. "Yes. He's actually awake and talking. The doctor was just discussing some of the next steps he'd like to take."

Philip let out a huge breath. "Good. Good." He grabbed Eve's hand. "Is it okay if we go in and see him?"

"The doctor suggests only one visitor at a time." She glanced at Eve and smiled. "He's been asking for you."

"He has?"

"I tried to call, but my phone has been completely useless, so I'm glad you came." Her smile widened. "Seeing you will brighten his day."

Eve didn't know how to respond to that.

After an awkward pause, Mackenzie added, "I think you should see him first." She pointed to a closed door on her right.

Eve looked at Philip, and he nodded.

She walked to the door and quietly turned the handle.

Roger was lying on his back, hands behind his head, looking at the ceiling.

He would've looked totally relaxed if it wasn't for the black and purple bruises covering the left side of his face and arm.

"Oh, Roger."

He whipped his head toward her and spread his arms wide. "Eve."

She ran to him, and he wrapped her in a bear hug. "I'm glad you came. I've been so worried about you."

She pulled out of the hug. "You were worried about me? I wasn't the one who was attacked." Tears filled her eyes. "I'm so sorry you and Mackenzie got pulled into this."

"Shhh." He patted her arm gently. "No need for any of that. Mackenzie already told me it took her hours to get Philip to stop apologizing the other day. But neither of you did anything wrong." He squeezed his eyes shut and maneuvered into a sitting position. He groaned and sat still for a few seconds before opening his eyes again. "You didn't come alone, did you? Is Philip here?"

"He's right outside the door with Mackenzie. He wanted to come in with me, but you're only allowed one visitor at a time. I can switch with him now if you like."

"Not yet." He swallowed. "First, I need to tell you something."

She pulled a chair close to the bed and sat. "Is it about you and Mackenzie being married? Or about you being a Christian?"

His lips tightened. "You know."

"I do, but I don't understand why you felt like you couldn't tell me either of those things."

"How did you find out?"

"I found out that you and Mackenzie were married on the day of the attack when I was told that your *wife* had insisted on riding in the ambulance with you. And the other day, Mackenzie shared with Philip that you had been attending church with her and that you'd recently given your life to Christ."

"You weren't supposed to find out that way." His voice was thick.

"How was I supposed to find out?"

"I was going to tell you that Mackenzie and I were married, but I …"

"But what?"

"But … nothing. Other than I kept putting it off, and I'm not sure why. And the longer I put it off, the more difficult it became."

"Did you think I would be upset that the two of you got back together?"

He waited a few seconds, then said. "I think that was part of it."

"Well, you were right. I would've been upset."

His head jerked back. "Really? Why?"

"The *why* is a bit complicated, and it took an emotional breakdown and a couple of deep conversations with Philip to get to the bottom of it." She sucked in the sterile hospital room air. Did she really just say all of that in one breath? She had more to say but instead, she gave Roger a tight grin. "I'll spare you the details."

"You had an emotional breakdown over Mackenzie and I being married?"

"It's more complicated than that, but what hurt the most was that you hid your marriage *and* your Christian faith from me. I thought we were friends, Roger."

"Eve, we've been friends way too long for you to doubt that."

"Well, what else was I supposed to think? You kept both Philip and me out of the loop. I felt like we were being tossed aside. I know your friendship with Philip is rocky, but not telling *me*? That hurt, Roger. It cut deep."

"I couldn't tell you about my newfound faith without telling you about Mackenzie." He sighed. "I was a coward. You dug deep into your feelings, even though it took going through a breakdown to do it." He shook his head. "For some reason, I couldn't find the capacity to do that. And I'm sorry. Please forgive me."

She clicked her tongue. "Of course, you're forgiven."

"Thanks. You know, a lot goes through your mind when

you're being stomped on, kicked, and beaten with a bat. Not to mention shot." He grimaced. "One of those thoughts was of me dying and you finding out about all of those things after I was dead. I made several promises to God that day. One of them was that if He allowed me to survive, I would make sure the two of us would have this conversation."

"Well, I'm glad you kept your promise. How many more did you make?"

He chuckled. "Several."

"Care to share?"

He blushed. "They all involve Mackenzie."

"Does she make you happy, Roger?"

The reddening in his cheeks deepened. "Very. I'm happier than I've been in a long, long time."

"Then congratulations on your new marriage. Or remarriage."

"New marriage is appropriate. Mackenzie and I are completely different from the people we were the first time around."

"I learned that about her as well. And judging from the way she greeted me in the waiting area, she's okay knowing that you and I were close to the altar ourselves."

"She is."

"I'm glad. I'm happy for the two of you, Roger. I really am."

He placed both of her hands in his. "Thank you."

There was a knock on the door, and Philip popped his head in. "Everything okay in here?"

She nodded, and so did Roger.

Philip stepped into the room, walked to the other side of Roger's bed, and stared at their hands. "I'm glad to see the two of you made up."

Roger shook his head. "I was never mad at her."

"No, but she was definitely mad at you."

"So, I've heard."

Eve released Roger's hand and looked at Philip. "I'm sorry. This took longer than I expected it to. I didn't mean to stay so long."

Philip waved away her comment. "I just wanted to make sure my friend still had his head attached."

She giggled and stood. "I'll let the two of you talk."

"Thanks for coming, Eve."

When she opened the door, Mackenzie stood in front of it. "Are you and Roger okay?" she asked.

Eve let the door float close behind her and motioned to the only two empty chairs in the waiting area. When they were seated, she replied, "Yes, we're okay."

Mackenzie whooshed out a breath. "Thanks for doing that. It was important for him to talk to you. He felt like he'd betrayed your trust by keeping our relationship a secret. It really bothered him."

"I'm glad we had the chance to clear the air," Eve leaned closer to her. "How are you doing?"

"Physically, I'm fine. Emotionally? It's been rough. The images of Roger being attacked still haunt me."

"I'm sorry you had to see that."

"Well, the good thing is, I was able to identify the men who did it, so that's what I've been trying to focus on."

"I think when Roger's released, that'll help as well."

"His doctors are surprised at how fast he's recovering. They think he may be able to go home in another week or so."

"He'll be glad to get back home."

"*Back* home?" She shook her head back and forth. "I think you're referring to the place where we *used* to live. No, we're not going back there. I would've never been able to sit in that kitchen again without reliving what happened."

"I didn't think about that, I'm sorry. Have you and Roger thought about where you'd like to go?"

"My family helped us find a new place. They're moving stuff out of the old one while I stay here with Roger."

"I hope it's not too far away."

"It's in the country. An older home off the Old River Road. Not far from Jack and Kite's place."

"Oh, that's not too far away at all. And the older homes

out there are really nice.”

“I love it. And it’s a lot bigger than the one we had before, with tons of space to set up another home studio.”

“He’s gonna love that.”

“Once we’re settled in, we’d love to have you and Philip over for dinner sometime.” She worried her lip. “I mean, if you don’t think it’ll be too awkward.”

“Um,” Eve racked her brain for the least abrasive way to ask the question she had in response to that. She couldn’t find one. “Roger was in love with me while you were married to him the first time. Does that not bother you?”

“No.” She shrugged. “Maybe it would if I had been a decent wife to him at the time.” She chuckled. “Heck, if I had even been a decent *person* maybe I’d have a few emotions about it. But I wasn’t. I fell in love with Roger the first time I laid eyes on him. We had something special, and we both knew it. However, I was too full of myself back then to treasure it. If I had been a better wife, he would’ve forgotten all about you.”

Ouch. Was that a dig? Or was that just Mackenzie’s way of bluntly responding to Eve’s just as blunt question?

Mackenzie grimaced. “That didn’t come out the way I wanted it to. What I’m trying to say is that I knew you and Roger were old friends, but when he first introduced us, I could tell by the way he looked at you, that you were more than just a friend to him. But I’m a firm believer that true love can conquer anything. Even a past love.”

Eve wasn’t sure that explanation helped Mackenzie in the way she’d hoped it would, but she had answered the question. Point taken. It didn’t bother her at all.

“I’ll have to talk to Philip, but I’m pretty sure he’ll be okay with accepting your dinner invitation.”

Mackenzie smiled. “Great. How about March 15th?”

That was almost six months away. And it was also Roger’s birthday.

Mackenzie chuckled. “Yes, that’s Roger’s birthday.” She motioned toward his hospital room. “But way before all of this happened, I asked him what he’d like to do for his birthday.

He said the only thing he wanted was a quiet dinner with his best friend and his best friend's wife. So, it'll just be the four of us. Does that sound okay?"

"It does."

"That also gives us plenty of time to settle in and for Roger to complete the physical therapy his doctor suggested."

Eve nodded, and Mackenzie laid a hand on her shoulder. "Thank you. Your friendship is important to Roger, and that makes it important to me. And through that, I'm hoping we'll become friends as well."

"I'd like that."

Mackenzie pulled her into a hug.

"Hey," Philip laughed softly. "What did I miss?"

She laughed with him, and so did Mackenzie.

"Just girl talk," Eve said.

"Ah, well, I'm afraid that has to come to an end." He looked at Mackenzie. "Your husband is asking for you."

Her face lit up. "I better go. Thank you both again for stopping by."

She stood and jogged the short distance to Roger's room.

Eve blew out a breath and stood next to Philip. "I didn't know how this visit would go, but I'm glad we came. I feel at peace now."

He kissed her forehead. "Good. You're gonna need it once we're back down in the lobby."

"Oh, right. The crowd. Those poor people. I hope they're not still waiting to see a doctor."

"I hope that, too." He winked at her. "But after that, it's just me and you, baby."

She giggled. "What in the world are you talking about?"

"The Corvette, remember?"

"You want to go on that long drive today?" She glanced at her watch. "There's only a couple of hours of daylight left."

"I know, that's why we need to hurry." He pushed the button for the elevator. "We pick up the Corvette from Dad's, then ride into the sunset."

"And what will we do when the sun sets?"

"Don't worry." His eyes twinkled. "I have plans for that, too."

Chapter 25

Angel Pines.

The private Stockton cabin overlooking Habakkuk Falls. Eve couldn't believe it.

She'd only been here twice before. The first time was on her very first date with Philip. He'd been a cocky teen back then who was more than eager to show Eve all his family had to offer. She'd been an impressionable, blushing teen at the time, and though he'd been disappointed that all he'd received that night was a kiss, the first evening they'd shared together had ended remarkably well.

Not so for the second time, she'd visited this cabin.

It'd been their tenth anniversary. She'd planned a romantic weekend getaway here at the cabin named after his grandmother, Angel Stockton.

She and Philip had gotten into an argument, and he stormed out, leaving her alone in the cabin.

On their anniversary.

She'd stayed and cried for hours, hoping he'd come back. He never did.

The next morning, she left and vowed never to return.

Philip brushed her shoulder, and she blinked her way out of the past.

"Evie, the last time we were here, it didn't end well. And I know you've never wanted to return because of that memory." He smiled. "But I'd like for us to make new memories here. Will you help me do that?"

His eyes were soft and twinkled like the stars above them. She didn't want to go inside that cabin. Memories of the stark loneliness and her bawling in the corner were sure to resurface.

But he said he wanted to replace those memories. She doubted he'd be successful, but he wanted to try.

Her heart warmed. How could she say no?

"Okay."

His smile widened. "Thank you."

They trekked through the tall grasses until they reached the cobblestone path leading to the cabin. Philip walked up the wooden steps before her, unlocked the door, and pushed it wide open.

The cabin glowed from the inside.

What in the world?

She stepped onto the porch, and he gently nudged her through the door.

There were candles everywhere. In the windows, on the mantle, the tables, and even lining the floor along the walls.

And roses. So. Many. Roses.

All of them red.

"Philip."

He took her hand and led her through the rest of the cabin, which only had two rooms plus a kitchen and a bathroom.

The fireplace was lit in the bedroom, and soft music played in the background. Her music. Love songs she'd written for her and Philip. Sung by her and other artists from the studio.

Songs she'd written long before the love she'd craved became a reality.

The bed was covered with a satin rose-colored duvet and plush white pillows.

Black pajamas with the face of a tiger on the pajama top

lay on one side of the bed.

And the skimpiest lacey white nightgown she'd ever seen lay on the other side.

She picked up the gown and giggled. "Really, Philip?"

He nodded and moaned. "I've been thinking about you in that nightie all day long."

Heat flushed her cheeks.

She turned to the bathroom. Besides a small vase on the counter with a single rose in it and more candles, it …

She stepped inside. Was that a massage table?

She walked over to the table and ran her fingers across the soft, plush towels on top of it. Not only was there a massage table, but along the rustic wooden counter next to it, was a vast array of massage oils, lotions, and a bottle of glistening liquid that promised to ….

"Philip Mark Stockton. You're a rascal, you know that?"

He chuckled and then looked at the bottle of liquid. "I'm going to give you a massage you'll never forget."

His eyes flicked to her. The look in them so sultry her legs wobbled.

She sat on the ledge of the bathtub. It was full of water, bubbles, and rose petals. She dipped a finger into the water. It was still hot. "I don't understand. When did you find the time to do all of this?"

"Everything you see was all my idea." He slid his hands into his pockets. "But I had a little help implementing it."

"Which one of my friends helped you?"

"Actually, it was Dinah and Kaloni."

"Dinah? And *Kaloni*? Your new-to-you daughter and sister?"

"Yeah. I texted Lydia and told her what I was thinking. The last time we were here it ended so badly that I … just wanted to make sure it would be received well by you. No one knows you better than Lydia, and I didn't want to cause any further pain." He sat on the ledge next to her. "She thought it was a wonderful idea and enlisted Dinah since she does stuff like this all the time at her event center."

Eve nodded. "Okay, that part makes sense, but how in the world does Kaloni fit into this? I thought she was going into the Witness Protection Program with her dad. I mean, *your* dad." She blew out a breath. "You know what I mean."

"She refused to go."

"Oh. Well, I can't say I blame her. She's young and from the South Pacific. I'm sure she'd feel much more at home there."

"Yeah, but somehow she found out about Dinah. I suspect from Lydia or Mary. She then decided to reach out to her niece, before boarding a plane back home."

"Really? How do you know all of this?"

"Kaloni called while I was in the hospital waiting room. We talked for a good while about Dad, her Mom, and mine. As well as the situation Dad had put us both in. She seems to be taking it in pretty well. We set up a time to meet, then she mentioned that she and Dinah had already met and were getting along well. She then said she was also in the hospitality business. She owns a hotel in Bora Bora called the Island Flower."

"That's the place Henderson told you to go to if he was still alive in three years."

"Yeah. Of course, I don't have to do that now since he surrendered to the FBI, but anyway, she then asked if she could help with your surprise. I told her I could use all the help I could get."

"Wow."

"I know."

"And Dinah? I mean, she loves her mom and would do anything Lydia asked, but in the past, she's drawn a red line when it came to anything involving you. Her agreeing to help is a big step for her."

"I suspect she did it more for you than me," he shrugged. "But that's okay. I'm glad Kaloni reached out to her, and they're getting along so well. I think that's going to help a lot when the three of us sit down to have those hard conversations."

Eve placed a hand on top of his. "It will."

He sucked in a breath and grinned. "I've been wanting to surprise you with this for a while and purchased the nightie and a couple of other items several weeks ago. Everything else, I picked out myself from a couple of websites Kaloni recommended. Thank goodness for rush delivery. I hope everything is to your liking."

"I love it." She scooped up a handful of bubbles from the tub and inhaled. "And everything is so fragrant. The bubbles in the bath, the oils, the lotions, the candles, and roses," she sniffed the air. "And I smell something else, too. Something sweet?" She sniffed again. "No, savory."

"That would be the lamb roasting in the oven. That's what you had prepared for us to eat on our tenth anniversary, right? Along with grilled asparagus, garlic potatoes, and a carrot soufflé?"

He remembered. Tears welled in her eyes. "Yes."

He twirled a strand of her hair around his finger. "I stormed out of here that night before I had the chance to enjoy you or that dinner." He swallowed. "I promise to never do that again."

He lifted her chin and kissed her tenderly before moaning and pulling away.

"So," he cleared his throat. "What would you like first? Food, massage, bath?"

Actually, she wanted the fourth option. The unspoken one.

His eyes danced. "Or we could start off with that one."

He pulled her tight against him and tugged at her sweater.

She swatted at his hands. "Now that I think about it, it'll probably be best if we start with food first."

"You sure?" He nibbled on her neck. When her moans mixed with his, she scooted away. Her body arched toward him in protest. "Yes, I'm sure. You went through a lot of trouble to do this tonight, and I want to enjoy all of it. Every single aspect of it. Even if it takes all night."

"All night?" He kissed her gently along her shoulders

before looking into her eyes. "No, love. I'm hungry. For both you and the food. Prepare yourself for a couple of days."

Chapter 26

Five days.

Eve stepped onto the wooden porch and smiled at the morning sky.

She'd just spent the best five days of her life in this cabin.

And if it was up to her, she'd spend many more. But life was calling. She had a café to re-open and employees and customers to contact.

Kay's Café would be open for business again soon.

But Philip's to-do list was more daunting than hers. Not only did he need to get back to running his company, he also needed to meet with his dad's lawyer. With Henderson only days away from officially entering the Witness Protection Program, there were a lot of legal things Henderson wanted Philip to take over, including several businesses and the Stockton estate.

And the FBI had arranged for Philip to see his father one last time before they relocated him.

Kaloni was able to refuse the protection, but even if Henderson wanted to, he couldn't. He'd already named names, and the FBI had started unwinding decades of political corruption.

Legion may be done with her and Philip, but Henderson

still had the wrath of *The Shadows* waiting for him. He knew there was no escaping that.

Unless he disappeared.

A gust of October wind blew cold drops of water her way from Habakkuk Falls. The majestic view and calming sounds of the waterfall were just a few hundred feet away from the cabin.

She tightened her scarf. Massive pines towered above the cabin and dotted the landscape. She could see why Philip's grandmother had loved this place so much, and why his grandfather had named it Angel Pines.

She mentally kicked herself for waiting so long to come back.

But she was also glad that she did. Philip had done what he'd set out to do. He'd given her new memories that completely overshadowed the old ones.

They'd laughed, teased, and played with each other in ways they never had before.

The refrigerator had been stocked with enough food to last them a month. He'd made sure Dinah and Kaloni included all of her favorites.

She'd eaten way too much and hoped the hikes they'd taken had burned away some of those calories.

But the more they hiked, the more she wondered about the wisdom of staying in a cabin so far away from civilization. They'd been told they had nothing further to worry about from G, but what if *Legion* wasn't done with them yet?

She posed that question to Philip, and he smiled and calmly said he'd taken care of that also.

Dinah and Kaloni weren't the only ones at the cabin before she'd arrived. Eitan had been also, and he'd set up an outside alarm and monitoring system.

He'd also left Philip a Walther PPQ 9mm pistol.

Her husband had thought of everything.

After their hikes, they lay in front of the fireplace, warmed up, and enjoyed each other's company. She still remembered the roaring fires, the scent of Philip's cologne, his touch …

She shivered. And it wasn't from the cold October wind.

The door behind her opened. Philip stepped onto the porch with the suitcase he'd secretly packed for their getaway. He jingled the keys to the Corvette. "Ready?"

"Yes, and no. Mostly no."

"We could always stay for another day or two."

She shook her head. "I want to, but it'll only be postponing the inevitable."

"You mean my meetings with my dad's lawyer, Dinah, and Kaloni."

"And just getting back to our lives."

"You know, " he slid the keys into his jeans pocket. "Financially we're in a good place. And once I take over Dad's estate, we'll be in an even better one. You don't have to open the café, and I don't have to go back to work. I could sell my half of the business to Harold, and you could retire. We could then kick our cares to the curb and spend the rest of our lives traveling and having fun together."

Where was all of this coming from? "Philip, all of that sounds like something you've been thinking about for a while."

"I have."

She looked out at the falls. Could it really be that simple?

Was a life of leisure something she even wanted? Did Philip even want that?

If he did, they could've done all of that years ago. They wouldn't have been able to live as leisurely as they could now, but still, they could've done it.

Maybe after the nightmare they'd just lived, he thought now would be a better time. But there was something about his tone that bothered her. There was a sadness to it she hadn't heard before.

She tapped his heart with her forefinger. "What's going on inside of there, Philip?"

He lowered his gaze. "Thoughts about Dad."

He didn't need to say anymore. After the arranged visit with Henderson in a few days, Philip wouldn't see, talk, or be able to communicate with his dad again.

Ever.

It was for Philip's protection as well as Kaloni's, and even though Henderson was guilty of a lot of things, Philip still loved him.

Henderson would never spend time in prison for killing his wife, and Philip had a lot of mixed emotions about that. He wanted justice for his mother, but his dad was eighty years old. Philip couldn't stand the thought of Henderson spending the remaining years of his life behind bars.

Fortunately, neither could Henderson's attorney. He'd convinced his client to sing like a canary. In return, he'd received immunity for his crimes.

Freedom for Henderson, not so much for Philip, who was suffering right in front of her eyes.

She wrapped her arms around his neck, and he lowered his forehead to meet hers. She kissed him softly and said, "I hate that you're having to go through this. And I'm struggling with forgiving Henderson for putting you in this position." A tear flowed down her cheek. "But don't forget that I'm here for you, okay? For anything you need. Promise me you won't forget that."

He wiped her tears away with his thumb. "I promise."

Chapter 27

Eve stepped out of the Corvette and onto her brick driveway.

A silver Ford Taurus sat next to the Corvette.

She smiled.

Lydia was here.

Philip grimaced. "I guess there's no better time than the present to start my apology tour."

Eve blinked. "You didn't do it when you called to get her advice about surprising me at the cabin?"

He shook his head. "I wanted to do it face to face. I owe her that."

"You don't have to do it. She's already forgiven you."

"I know." He closed the driver's side door and locked it with the remote. "But she and I still need to talk." He retrieved their suitcase from the trunk. "It's a conversation that's long overdue."

She followed Philip to the door. Much to Philip's disdain, she'd given Lydia keys to their home long ago. In the past, he yelled at both of them about it, but Lydia ignored his rants and retorted that until he treated his wife better, she would always insist on having access to their house. He tried changing the locks once, but when he realized Eve would keep giving Lydia an extra set of keys, he gave up.

Fortunately, today, he didn't seem to mind.

The front door flew open, and Lydia beamed at them. "The lovebirds have returned."

She stepped aside for them to enter, then dropped keys into Eve's hand. "These no longer work." She nodded to the house across the street. "Eitan let me inside."

Oh, she'd forgotten that Eitan and Gila had installed locks that worked in conjunction with the new high-tech alarm system.

Lydia chuckled. "Good thing he saw me pull up. I would've been so embarrassed if the two of you returned home only to see me being hauled away in handcuffs."

The three of them chuckled.

Lydia pointed to the kitchen table. "Are you guys hungry? I made sandwiches."

They'd snacked on food from the cabin refrigerator on the four-hour drive home, but the sandwiches Lydia made looked delicious.

Philip placed the suitcase on the floor. "Sure, but first I'd like to talk to you for a second if that's okay?"

The shock on Lydia's face almost made Eve giggle. Philip had never asked to speak to Lydia alone before.

At least, not since he'd been married to Eve.

Lydia glanced at her, and she nodded.

Lydia responded with a quirked eyebrow.

Eve returned her quirk with a smile. "It's okay. He honestly just wants to talk. He's not going to yell, I promise."

"He knows his yelling doesn't scare me." Lydia narrowed her eyes at Philip. "Is this about you being Dinah's father?"

"That ... and some other things."

She stared at him for a few seconds before agreeing.

They sat at the kitchen table, and Eve headed to their bedroom. She tossed her purse on a chair and plopped down on the bed. When her eyes blurred from staring at the floor, she closed them. *Lord, Philip, and Lydia have a lot of history to unpack. Give Philip words that won't reopen old wounds. And may today be the day that Lydia's absolutely convinced that Philip has changed for the better.*

Of all her friends, she was glad Lydia was the first he'd talk to. Lydia's heart had already softened toward him. Not because of anything he'd done, but because the bitterness in her own heart toward Philip had threatened to become an obstacle in her friendship with Eve.

She hadn't seen Lydia in weeks, and she wasn't surprised her friend had been here waiting for them to return, especially since she was the one who helped pull Eve from the grips of depression after her and Philip's last visit to the cabin.

Lydia had probably expected Philip to grunt and disappear like he usually did when she visited.

She hadn't been expecting a conversation.

Or perhaps she had. She'd made sandwiches for Philip as well, but no doubt she'd expected the conversation to be casual and kind since she'd helped him with the surprise.

But no way would she have been expecting an apology.

Eve fluffed one of the pillows and laid her head on it. She was so proud of her husband. Instead of running from the bad decisions he'd made in his past, he was facing them head-on.

He truly was becoming the man of her dreams.

Her pocket buzzed, and her heart skipped a beat. She hoped it wasn't Lydia calling to say she was leaving. Surely things couldn't have gone that wrong that fast?

She yanked her phone free from her pocket and stared at the name.

Kite.

O me of little faith. "Lord, please forgive me for once again doubting the work You've done in my husband's life."

She tapped the answer button. "Hello there, Mrs. Eagle."

Kite chuckled. "Well, don't you sound awfully cheerful this afternoon. I take it the past few days with Philip went well."

"Oh, yes."

Kite giggled. "I hope you know I can feel you blushing

through the phone."

"I'm just glad you didn't decide to video call me. Otherwise, my face would've shown you a lot more than blushed cheeks. Everything Philip and I did would've been written all over it."

"Oh, so your time together didn't just go well, it went *really* well."

"Yeah." She tried not to stretch out the word, but her mouth did it anyway.

"I'm so glad, Eve. The two of you have been through a lot lately. You deserved some time away."

"Thanks. You know, I thought we were handling the situation with Henderson and Garringer well but it wasn't until we got the chance to be fully alone that I realized just how wound up we both were."

"Rest and relaxation is the best medicine. That's one of the reasons I'm calling. Now that you and Philip have had some time alone, your friends would like some time with the two of you, too. The weather's supposed to be nice this weekend, and I'm planning a picnic. I would love it if you and Philip would come."

"So, it's not just the ladies?"

"No, the guys have been complaining about how much time we spend together without them, so I decided to let them join in on the fun. However, I'm starting to regret it. Jack and Barry are already talking about playing some kind of football game where they tag each other."

"Philip loves tag football."

"Good. It'll be at a park. Steady will also be there, and Ethan as well. Plus, a couple of guys from church. It'll be fun."

"I can't wait to tell him."

"Also, Ted will be there."

Ted Eller was a college friend of Kite's husband Jack. She and Philip had only met Ted and his wife, Jan, a few times, but they'd gotten along pretty well.

Kite added, "I'm really glad the Ellers will be joining us. You and Jan have more in common than you realize."

"We do? Like what?"

Kite let out a heavy sigh. "She knows Garringer."

"What?"

"I don't know all the details yet, but from what she's shared with me, it sounds like her aunt used to belong to one of his cults."

"Are you serious?"

"Yes, and she's already told Sgt. Dodge what she knows. When they showed Garringer's picture on the news the night of the warehouse shootout, she said she almost had a heart attack."

"Why?"

"She thought he was dead."

"Dead?" Eve's mind swam with confusion. "What made her think that?"

"Because she was there the night her friend set his body on fire."

Chapter 28

Eve shut the passenger door behind her and looked out across the park.

Kite was right. It was a beautiful day for a picnic.

"What all did you put in here, woman?"

Philip held their picnic basket in front of him. "This thing weighs a ton. How much food did you put in here?"

"Oh, it's not just food. There are also the five bottles of sparkling grape juice I added, plus the water glasses, ceramic plates, silverware—"

"Plates and silverware? You didn't bring paper items?"

She frowned. "Of course not."

He chuckled. "I think Priscilla has been a bad influence on you."

"Believe it or not, it was probably Mom. When I was younger, we used to go on picnics all the time with Dad. And Mom always used tableware, never plasticware or paper."

"Yeah, well, your mom has always been kind of hoity-toity."

"You're such a snot."

He placed the wicker basket on the ground and swooped her up into his arms. She threw her head back and laughed as he swung her around, and the wind teased at her pleated skirt.

"Philip," she breathed out between giggles. "You have to put me down. I have on a skirt."

He looked into her eyes. "The sun is bright, and the sky is blue, but even in all their glory, they can't compare to you."

"Oh, you're a poet now?"

"I've been playing around with it. Whaddya think? Should I keep my day job?"

"It wasn't *too* bad. Maybe you could work part-time."

He lowered her to the ground. "You're the best thing that's ever happened to me you know that?"

He'd never said those words to her before. She ran her fingers through his hair. "I know now."

He lifted her chin, kissed her, then whispered, "I love you, Mrs. Stockton."

"I love you too, *Mr.* Stockton."

"Ahem."

Jack and Kite walked up to them. "Are we interrupting?" Kite asked with a huge grin.

Philip took Eve's hand. "Actually—"

She nudged him with her elbow. He winked at her then turned to Jack. "Good to see you again."

"Likewise." Jack motioned toward a field on the other side of the pavilion. "You're on my team. Hope you've been practicing."

They walked toward the men playing on the field. Kite turned to Eve. "You know, for the first time since I've known him, I can honestly say, I think your Philip fellow is a nice guy."

"I'm glad you're starting to see what I've been seeing." Eve's heart was blessed by Kite's comment. Like the rest of her girlfriends, Kite had grown up in Habakkuk. None of them had met Philip until high school, but Kite hadn't liked him back then, either. And to hear one of her dearest friends say he was a nice guy meant the world to her. And she was the second one in a week to compliment Philip.

His conversation with Lydia had gone better than any of them thought it could. After they hashed out their past issues, Lydia told her that she now considered Philip a friend and not just the husband of a friend.

Tears pricked at her eyes. For so long she'd been embarrassed by Philip's behavior around her friends. The fact that she no longer had to apologize or explain away his quick temper and crude remarks toward her, was a huge weight off her shoulders.

"Eve," Kite tilted her head to the side. "You still with me?"

"I'm sorry." She blinked to keep the tears in the well. "I was just thinking about what you said about Philip. It means a lot to me."

Kite pulled her into a hug. "I meant every word."

"Thank you."

Kite grabbed one of the handles on the picnic basket and Eve the other. Kite pointed to a pavilion to their left at the end of a long concrete path.

The pavilion was buzzing with people, but she couldn't quite make out all the faces.

"Everybody's already here," Kite said as they started walking. "Windy and Anthony are here, too. Somewhere. I think they went for another spin on his motorcycle."

"I haven't seen your sister in ages. I'm glad she's here."

"I am, too." Kite sucked in a breath. "I love Anthony, he's good for her. However, I wish she didn't ride with him on his motorcycle so much. Even though we're both adults, I still feel like the over-protective big sister. But as she constantly likes to remind me, there's only a few minutes separating us."

"I know she chides you about that, but I'm sure she appreciates you looking out for her more than she lets on."

"I hope so. I only want the best for her." Kite pointed at the pavilion again. "Let's see, Barry and Pris are here, so are the Days, the Melsons, the Isaacs, and the Rabins."

The Melsons, Isaacs, and Rabins were all a part of Mary's huge family but getting used to hearing her friend Lydia referred to by her new last name of Day, still took some getting used to. She married Steady Day almost two years ago, but for fifty-plus years, Eve had only known her as Lydia Dooley.

"Ted and Jan Eller are here as well."

Eve swallowed. She knew Jan was eager to talk with her about Garringer, but did it have to be today? She regretted agreeing to it. The day was going so well, and she didn't want to ruin it by talking about Garringer.

But she liked Jan. A lot. And she'd never come across as flaky or flighty. So, if she had some additional knowledge about Garringer, it was probably best to hear her out. Especially since the police and FBI hadn't been able to find out anything new regarding his whereabouts.

As they got closer, Eve recognized several other faces. Pastor Greene and Ruth were there, as well as a few other members of their church. J.S., also known as Jack's Shadow, was there, the young man Jack Eagle had taken under his wings several years ago, and standing next to him was his fiancé Xenia.

As soon as she and Kite lifted the heavy basket and placed it on the nearest table, she was greeted with hugs, kisses, and tons of *"we're-so-glad-you-and-Philip-are-okay."*

She greeted and chatted with them before glancing around the huge concrete and wooden structure. Kite had chosen the most sought-after pavilion at Spring Bluff State Park.

Not only was it large enough to host big groups, but it was surrounded by Downy Serviceberry trees and an array of ornamental grasses planted along a narrow footpath that ended at a small lake.

It usually took months to reserve this spot. She had no idea how Kite managed to secure it on such short notice.

"Hi." Jan Eller came around from behind her.

"Hey." Eve really needed to ask Jan what hair products she used. Her dark brown hair was always so shiny and pretty.

Jan pointed to a picnic table in the corner that no one had claimed yet. "Do you mind if we go over there and talk?"

Eve followed her to the table and sat next to Jan on the bench.

"I know you and Philip just got here, and it's a beautiful day, and everyone is having such a good time," she blew out a breath. "And if I didn't think it was important, I wouldn't bring this up today." She stared at her hands before continuing. "But I'd rather talk now so later we'll be able to focus on just having fun this afternoon. Is that okay?"

Eve leaned against the table. "Sounds like a good idea."

"First, I want to say how sorry I am for everything you and Philip had to go through. I know everything turned out okay, but I also know how much of an emotional toll it can take."

Eve remembered thinking the same thing at the cabin. "Yeah, I guess when you're in the thick of it you don't think about it too much. You just focus on survival. But afterward is when it kind of hits you."

"Exactly. How are you guys doing now?"

"Pretty good. We went away for a few days to a little cabin we own. We were able to talk about the situation and relieve some stress. It helped a lot."

"I'm glad to hear that." She scratched her cheek. "There are only a handful of people in Habakkuk who know about my past with Garringer. Kite is one of them, and I only told her about it a few days ago. It's not something I want widely known. I don't want my name or my family's to be tied to his."

"How do you know Garringer?"

"My parents died when I was young, and I was sent to live with my aunt in Corinth. She was in a Satanic cult, and Garringer was their leader."

"When was this?"

"Early eighties."

"You said he was in Corinth. As in Corinth, Missouri?"

"Yes. That's one of the things I immediately notified Sgt. Dodge about because he and the FBI were under the impression that he was from Oregon, but he's not."

Eve's heart skipped a beat. Corinth was only an hour east of Habakkuk. "You're sure?"

"Trust me, the time I spent in Corinth is something I'll never forget."

"Were you … a part of the cult?"

"No, but Garringer desperately wanted me to be, and he was almost successful at dragging me into it. " She shivered. "That's a long story, but I just wanted you to know that Garringer's powerful, in the spiritual sense. I've witnessed him place curses on people and cause them *and* the things around them to levitate. He's also a rapist and a murderer. He killed my best friend's mother."

"Oh, Jan."

"The last time I saw Garringer, he was severely injured, and my friend, the daughter of the woman he killed, doused him with gasoline. That whole night was a nightmare. My aunt made sure I made it out of the house before it blew up." She shook her head. "So, when I saw Garringer's picture on the news, I was shocked. He looked the same as he did forty years ago. I'd recognize that monster anywhere." She shuddered again. "I just wanted you and your family to be aware of who you're dealing with. Stayed prayed up. If he isn't the devil incarnate, I don't know who is."

Eve closed her eyes and tried to wrangle just one of the questions flying around her brain. When she was mentally able to grab one, she asked, "Do you think Philip and I are out of danger?"

Jan clasped her hands together on top of the table. After a few seconds, she said, "For now, yes. I think he was summoned by whomever or whatever away from here. They like to work in the dark. They don't want people to know they exist, and with all the news coverage surrounding the warehouse incident, I think it'll be a long time before he manifests again in Habakkuk." She looked Eve in the eyes. "But again, that's why I wanted to have this conversation. Just because Garringer's been spotted in another state, doesn't mean he can't cause harm. His most powerful weapon is the spiritual world. I just wanted to tell you to stay alert, and realize you're in a spiritual war, not a physical one."

Eve reached for Jan's hands and held them. It was obvious there was a lot more Jan wasn't sharing about her time with the cult or Garringer. It was written all over her face, and in the hands that were trembling inside hers.

Whatever she had seen or been through had scarred her deeply.

She mentioned that she'd been able to escape the night he died. Or the night she thought he died. Eve wondered if Garringer saw Jan before she had the chance to flee.

And if that was part of the reason he was back in Missouri. Habakkuk specifically.

Jan's husband had been an evangelist before becoming pastor of a small Habakkuk church. They'd recently decided to settle here. Before that, the Eller family had traveled extensively, even internationally.

But now they were close to where Jan's nightmare with the cult started.

Did Garringer know Jan was back in Missouri?

Had he intended to kill two birds with one stone? Complete the mission he'd been given regarding her and Philip and then go after Jan?

She had no idea, but she had the feeling Jan might've been wondering the same thing.

Eve closed her eyes again. Lydia and Mabel were the spiritual warriors, not her. But that was okay. God had brought her too far to fear now.

She prayed for Godly wisdom, for her family and Jan's. She also asked that He'd continue to protect them from an enemy who'd targeted them both.

Eve smiled as she remembered a pastor from her childhood who often said, *if you're not a target of the enemy, that's a problem. That means he already owns you or he doesn't see you as a threat. However, if he's shooting fiery darts your way, then you're doing something right and the demons in hell are mad.*

"Thanks for that prayer," Jan sucked in a deep breath and blew it out. Her voice wasn't as shaky as before. "And thanks for listening. Sometimes I forget not to get so wrapped up in the past. It takes my focus off God. But I felt it was important to share what I knew about Garringer. And for you and Philip to continue to Ephesians 6:10-16 your lives."

The Armor of God Scriptures. "Will do. And thanks for thinking of us."

She pulled Jan into an embrace, and then heard greetings and laughter from the front of the pavilion.

She turned and saw Dinah had arrived, and Kaloni was with her. After Dinah introduced Kaloni to everyone, a man stepped up behind Dinah and wrapped an arm around her waist.

Was that Eitan?

She squinted to get a better look. It didn't work. But there was no doubt that was Eitan.

Were he and Dinah a *couple?*

When did that happen?

Jan gave her a slight nudge. "I guess it's time we go mingle."

Eve stood, then added, "One day I'd like to hear the rest of the story regarding your time with Garringer."

"And one day I might tell it." She smiled. "Perhaps one day soon."

"Promise?"

"Promise."

They joined the others who were gathered around the picnic tables near the front. The guys were still playing football on the field, so Philip hadn't yet noticed Kaloni and Dinah.

She and Philip met Kaloni for the first time a few days ago at the law firm representing their dad. Afterward, Philip took Kaloni out for a long lunch.

Kaloni sat at the table next to Lydia. Her ebony hair was parted in the middle and flowed down the back of her sleeveless dress. Her blue eyes stood out against her golden-bronze skin. She was a standout in any crowd.

Eve couldn't believe she now had a sister-in-law.

She walked behind Kaloni and gave her a squeeze. "I didn't know you were coming."

"I didn't, either." Kaloni turned to Eve. Her teeth were as white as the beautiful dress she wore. "Dinah invited me out to lunch." She pointed to her dress. "I had no idea she meant a picnic lunch."

Eve laughed. "Sounds like something Dinah would intentionally omit."

"Yeah, I'm starting to find that out. Where's Philip?"

"He's with his team somewhere practicing for the big game."

"What game?"

"Oh, it's just tag football." Eve sat next to her. "But to them, it's a big deal."

Kaloni smiled. "I'm not sure what tag football is, but I'm looking forward to cheering for my big brother."

"Me too." Eve looked across the park as the men jogged their way. "Oh, look. Here they come now."

The men ran up to the picnic tables and immediately began devouring the food the women had set out.

Philip greeted Kaloni and sat next to them. Eve asked, "Is the game over?"

He swallowed the huge chunk of hot dog he'd bitten off. "No, we're about to start."

"When?"

"Now, that's why we're eating so fast."

"Well, you need to slow down. Eating that fast is not good for the digestive system. As a matter of fact, I'm not sure you should be eating at all before you go back out there." She handed him a bottle of water.

"I need all the energy I can get. Jack's the captain of our team, and I want to make sure Barry's team eats dust. They've been talking smack to us all afternoon. I gotta be ready to bring the smoke."

The what?

She giggled. She had no idea what Philip was talking about, and she was pretty sure he didn't either. But at least he was having fun.

After everyone enjoyed food from each other baskets, the men headed back to the grassy field in front of the pavilion.

Eve watched as Philip darted here and there and ran with the ball. It was the first time she could remember seeing Philip run. He'd wrestled some in high school, but that was about it. She and Kaloni cheered him on as the other team tried to catch him. They eventually did, but it took a while.

Her heart burst with pride.

She watched and laughed with the others as everyone cheered on their favorites. They were loud, and there was lots of teasing, but in the end, Jack's team pulled off the win.

As the guys cleaned their hands before digging back into the food, she reached into her basket and pulled out the two blankets she'd packed. The sun was about to set, and she wanted to spend time by the lake before it did.

When Mabel handed Philip a plate of apple cobbler, Eve whispered in his ear, "I'm going to sit by the lake for a bit."

He held up a finger and swallowed a forkful of cobbler. "Hold on. I'll go with you."

"The app on my phone says the sun will set in forty-five minutes. I just want to enjoy as much of the scenery at the lake as I can before it gets dark. Take your time and celebrate your win. You were great out there. And when you're done, come join me."

"You sure you don't mind?"

"I don't mind at all."

He gave her a peck on the lips. "Love you."

"Love you, too."

She stopped by the table where Kite, Lydia, and Pris were and told them where she was going.

She walked down the narrow path to the lake, dropped one of the blankets on the grass, and spread the other on the ground. She kicked off the sandals that were definitely not made for a cool autumn day and sat on the blanket. She tucked her feet under her skirt, and her toes deep into the blanket.

Spring Bluff State Park was a favorite for many in Habakkuk because it was off the beaten path. It was significantly smaller than other state parks in the area and lacked some of the major amenities parkgoers enjoyed, but it made up for that with its natural beauty.

On the right side of the lake was a packed gravel trail with several couples walking along it. Many of the couples were from the pavilion up the hill from theirs, but Mary and Ethan were also on the trail, holding hands, smiling, and whispering to each other.

Mary's giggles echoed across the lake.

To her left was a footbridge, with twinkling lights underneath, that ended at the water's edge. From there, parkgoers could hike a short trail that led to an exceptional view of the Ozark Mountains.

Eve stared across the calming and serene lake view in front of her. She loved this spot, her own personal oasis from the world. She'd spent many early mornings and late afternoons here, praying, writing songs, singing, crying.

But the worries she had back then, and the fears she previously had about Garringer, seemed to shimmer on top of the water in front of her and disappear into its depths.

What floated to the top was a joy so sweet she could taste it.

So much had happened. Everything from Mr. Hale to Roger, and all of the surprises, upheavals, and turmoil in-between.

But God had handled them all.

And He'd even managed to release her and Philip from their emotional prisons.

She thanked God for His awesomeness and smiled at the noise traveling down the hill toward her.

Their group had been loud when they'd cheered on the men, but the group up the hill from them had been even louder. She had no idea what they were celebrating, but whatever it was, they were pretty excited about it.

Priscilla's laugh filled the air. She'd recognize Pris's hearty laugh anywhere, so merriment was still happening with her friends at their pavilion as well.

She'd rejoin them later, but right now, she wanted to enjoy the moment.

For years she'd wanted her and Philip to attend outings like these together, but she'd end up going alone. And no matter how hard she tried, she couldn't stop herself from watching other couples interact.

And envying them.

But today, she had been one of those couples.

Their interactions had flowed so naturally. It was evident that Philip not only loved her, but he was *in* love with her as well.

It was in the way he looked at her. Mostly, the looks were loaded with warmth, longing, and passion. But there were other times where they were full of kindness, reassurance, playfulness, and love.

His touches were always so tender. And she loved the way he'd take her hand, kiss it gently, pull her close, and sigh as though nothing else mattered at that moment.

And oh. The way he nibbled her neck …

"Hey darling."

Darling? That one was new. She smiled. The list of affectionate names that he'd began calling her was growing.

Philip unfolded the blanket she'd dropped on the grass earlier and wrapped it around her. "You seem lost in your thoughts," he tucked in a corner of the blanket. "Mind sharing them with me?"

He smelled of spicy BBQ sauce and Italian seasonings. Smudges of sauce were on his cheek, chin, and T-shirt. "What in the world have you been eating?"

He snuggled next to her. "Mabel brought meatballs." He looked down at his T-shirt. For a minute she thought he was going to lick the sauce off of it. "They're so good. I'm addicted. I think I might need a support group."

"One has already been started at the café. They meet on Thursdays at seven p.m."

He turned toward her. "Really?"

She shook her head and laughed.

"Oh, I see." He tickled her sides. "You almost had me there for a second."

"I have my moments."

"By the way," his brows furrowed. "Mabel has this amazing thing that keeps food steaming hot like it just came from the oven. I'd like for us to start having picnics together, just the two of us here by the lake. Tomorrow, let's go shopping and get you some of those things that keep food hot."

"Yes, to us having lakeside picnics. No, to the shopping trip."

"Why?"

"Because we already have several warmers like that."

"We do?"

"Yeah, they're on the top shelf of the kitchen pantry."

"Oh." He lowered his eyes. After a long pause, he said, "You know, I'm embarrassed that I've missed so many of the little things like that in our home, in our lives," he swallowed. "With you." He looked at her. "It's sad, but at the same time, I feel like I'm seeing everything for the *first* time. The cozy way you've decorated and taken care of our home, and the decades of prayer that fill it." He inched closer. "I'm no longer going to take any of that for granted. I'm a Christian man with a new outlook on life—because of you and your prayers. You didn't run off when you had the chance. You stayed and prayed."

"I certainly did a lot of praying, but it was the Holy Spirit who changed your heart."

"I know." He nodded. "But it was you who sought Him continually on my behalf." He chuckled. "As a matter of fact, you may have been the *only* one." His face turned serious again. "And I want to take this moment to say thank you, love. Thank you, for everything."

Tears filled her eyes. "I'm your helpmeet, remember? I only did what I was supposed to do."

"With the way I treated you? No. You went above and beyond. In the bad times and very bad times, you stuck with me. Through thick and thin, just like you vowed to all those years ago."

"Yeah," she shuddered. "We have been through a lot."

"That's what I was trying to say earlier. It was rough, but somehow it brought us closer together. We've shared things with each other that we've kept sheltered inside our hearts for years. We were able to let all of that go and become knitted together in the process. I don't know," he shrugged." But to me, there's beauty in that."

"As in, the Lord gave us beauty for the ashes?"

"And the oil of joy for mourning." He smiled. "Isaiah 61:3. That's exactly what I meant."

"Joy. That's what I'm feeling right now."

"Me too." He ran his fingers through her hair. "It feels like silk."

"Thank you."

"And your eyes. Such a beautiful brown. I don't think I've ever seen anything like them before."

"Philip," she chastised. "You've been looking into these eyes for over thirty years."

"As I said, it's like I'm seeing everything for the first time." He tossed the blanket aside and caressed her arm. "And you have the softest skin." He kissed her wrist." I can't stop touching it." He looked up at her. "And those lips, they're so darn kissable and intoxicating that I just wanna—"

Fireworks exploded in the sky. Eve squinted at the burst of color above them. "Did Kite say anything about setting off fireworks?"

Silence.

She turned to look at him. He wasn't even looking at the sky. He was still staring at her lips.

"Philip?"

"The fireworks are from the group up on the hill."

"That's against the rules. Fireworks are not allowed in the park."

"I know," he picked up the blanket again and spread it over them. "But I'm glad they're doing it." He cupped her chin and looked deep into her eyes. "It's the perfect visual for the way I'm feeling inside right now."

When his lips touched hers, a soft glow from the fireworks surrounded them. With each pop of the pyrotechnic display, he kissed her deeper.

And deeper.

She moaned.

So did he.

She didn't want to do it, but she had to pull away. If she didn't, there was no telling what kind of trouble they'd find themselves in under the blanket.

She looked at Philip. His eyes reflected the colors exploding in the sky.

He groaned, then placed her head on his shoulder.

The lake in front of them mirrored the red, orange, and silver firework showers falling upon it. As well as the coppery rays of the setting sun.

Lydia and Kite called her name and Philip's.

No doubt they were warning them that park rangers were on site ready to shoo them all away.

Oh, well. She'd wait until they showed up.

Until then, she was going to continue to bask in the love of her husband and watch the sun set behind the beautiful Ozark Mountains.

And maybe sneak in another kiss before it did.

------- THE END -------

KARA R. HUNT is the host of the Cheer UP! Podcast and an award-winning author.

Her novels have received the 2023 Golden Scrolls Award for Contemporary Novel of the Year and the coveted 2023 Selah Award for Contemporary Womens Fiction.

Kara is an avid reader and usually can be found reading a novel from one of her favorite authors or listening to one of their audiobooks.

Kara and her husband reside in rural Missouri.

SOCIAL MEDIA LINKS

Website: https://kararhunt.com/

Goodreads: https://www.goodreads.com/user/show/2610898-kara-r-hunt

Facebook: https://www.facebook.com/AuthorKaraRHunt

Instagram: https://www.instagram.com/kararhunt/

Twitter: AuthorKaraRHunt